BONJOUR, KELLY!

The windows of the café were hung with heavy red velvet drapes, and it took Kelly's eyes a moment to adjust to the darkness. When she recovered her sight, she saw Eric immediately, sitting in a corner of the room near the kitchen. But he was sitting with . . . Nathalie!

"Kelly!" Eric jumped up when he saw her. "I thought you couldn't get away for lunch. What a surprise! But how did you know where to find us?"

"It wasn't too hard," Kelly replied coolly, looking at Nathalie. "Though I am surprised to see you here."

Nathalie laughed good-naturedly. "Really, Kelly, this isn't one of those soap operas you Americans are forever watching. There's nothing sneaky going on here." She smiled at Eric. "Is there, *chéri*?"

Bantam Books in the Kelly Blake, Teen Model series
Ask your bookseller for the books you have missed

#1 *DISCOVERED!*
#2 *RISING STAR*
#3 *HARD TO GET*
#4 *HEADLINERS*
#5 *DOUBLE TROUBLE*
#6 *PARIS NIGHTS*

●●●●●●●●●**6**●●●●●●●●●
KELLY BLAKE
TEEN MODEL
●●●●●●●●●●●●●●●●●●●●●

Paris Nights

Yvonne Greene

BANTAM BOOKS
TORONTO • NEW YORK • LONDON • SYDNEY • AUCKLAND

RL 6, IL age 12 and up

PARIS NIGHTS
A Bantam Book / January 1987

*Setting of back-cover photo of Kelly Blake in the soda shoppe
courtesy of Antique Supermarket.*

ISBN 0-553-26199-1

Published simultaneously in the United States and Canada

Bantam Books are published by Bantam Books, Inc. Its trademark, consisting of the words "Bantam Books" and the portrayal
of a rooster, is Registered in U.S. Patent and Trademark Office
and in other countries. Marca Registrada. Bantam Books, Inc.,
666 Fifth Avenue, New York, New York 10103.

PRINTED IN THE UNITED STATES OF AMERICA

O   0 9 8 7 6 5 4 3 2 1

Paris Nights

One

The offices of the FLASH! modeling agency were bustling with Christmas preparations when Kelly Blake stopped by late one December afternoon. Debby, the receptionist, was busy putting out poinsettia plants, while several of the agency messengers struggled with a huge Christmas tree.

"Hey, Kelly!" Debby greeted her. "Looking forward to your vacation from school?"

"Oh, sure," Kelly replied. She tried to sound as cheerful as the surroundings demanded, but inside she didn't feel a bit of Christmas joy. Nothing had held any joy for her since her boyfriend, Eric Powers, had told her he wouldn't be around for the holidays.

"That's just great!" Debby grinned. "I'm already over my head in debt and I haven't even gotten through half my Christmas shopping!"

"Well, I hope Santa makes it up to you," was about all Kelly could think to reply. The person she really wanted to talk to was her booker, Nina. Maybe, if she was extra lucky, she could get some of the rare bookings for the holidays. If she kept really busy she wouldn't notice the fun all her friends would be having.

"Is Nina in, Deb?" she asked.

"Uh-huh. She's on about four phone calls, but why don't you go on in." Deb waved and turned to answer a ringing phone.

Nina sat behind a cluttered desk, a phone to her ear and a pile of charts in front of her. Blinking lights on her telephone indicated that several people were on hold. As soon as one model or client had been helped, another called in. Nina turned to greet Kelly with an exasperated look. Five o'clock in the agency was torture, Kelly knew. Yet, as much as she sympathized with Nina, she could barely sit still while her booker took care of the calls.

"Hi, honey." Nina glanced in her direction briefly. "Can I help you?"

"Yes, I . . ." Kelly began. But Nina had turned away. "I'm sorry," she was saying, "but we have to charge you time and a half for bookings after five-thirty. What? Yes, I understand that the film was spoiled. Yes. But that's not the model's fault. No, I can't make an exception. As it is, Casey had to miss an important television appointment. No, I'm sorry, I have to charge you. Would you like to speak to Meg Dorian? Hold on, I'll switch you."

Sighing, she turned to Kelly once more. "What is it, hon? Would you like to see your chart for this week?"

"Well," Kelly began, "I was thinking that . . ."

But she'd lost Nina again. "What?" the booker was yelling into the phone, her voice sounding hoarse and tired. "Where are you, Kim? In California? Don't you know you have a booking back here at nine o'clock tomorrow morning? What? Yes, I certainly do suggest you take the next flight back to New York tonight. What about your eyes? Eyedrops, Kim, eyedrops. I'd better see you back here first thing tomorrow, sleep or no sleep. You can make up for it over the holidays."

Exhausted, she turned back to Kelly. "Now, honey—what is it you were trying to ask me?"

Kelly didn't quite know where to begin. "I was just thinking. I hate to turn down any work. I could take jobs over Christmas—anything at all!"

Nina stared at her. "Why don't you stick to your decision and enjoy your vacation? You'll work plenty after New Year's—you just enjoy Christmas and all those parties and"—she winked at Kelly—"that fellow of yours."

Once again the phone rang, and Nina turned away. Kelly was afraid the subject was closed. This called for drastic action. She hadn't come all the way into New York for nothing! Taking a deep breath, she walked around the corner into the private office of Meg Dorian, the head of the agency.

"Kelly! What a nice surprise!" Meg said. "Less than a week before Christmas and still so much commotion! Can't a woman get a little peace?"

As Kelly shut the office door, Meg's intercom buzzed.

"Just a minute, Kelly," Meg said. "What is it?" she asked crisply into the intercom.

"It's Patrick, the photographer for the Bonjour people," Nina's voice answered. "He's worried about the model we booked for their big job. Says she's gained some weight since he saw her portfolio."

"Put Patrick on the line," Meg said wearily. She glanced up at Kelly. "Was there something you wanted?"

"Uh, just to say Merry Christmas," Kelly began.

The intercom buzzed and Meg snatched up her telephone. "Merry Christmas to you, too." She waved Kelly away. "Hello, Patrick? Can you hear me? The connection's not very good here." Seeing Kelly still standing by her desk, Meg frowned. "Just a minute, Patrick. Kelly, this is an overseas call. Would you mind?"

"No, of course not." Kelly backed out of the office.

"Shut the door, please," Meg called after her.

Nina looked up as Kelly passed her desk on the way out. "Hey, cheer up," she said. For a moment, the phones were silent. "Why so glum? You don't really want to work, do you? I thought you were thrilled to be free for that big dance, and parties with your boyfriend—uh-oh." Nina gave her an understanding look. "Boyfriend trouble. I can spot it a mile away."

Kelly dropped into the chair by Nina's desk. She felt so dispirited she was afraid she might cry. "Everything's terrible," she moaned. "I came home from that Texas job to find that Eric's going to Paris with his family for two whole weeks over Christmas. All our plans are ruined. He'll be having fun in Paris, and I'll be stuck at home."

"Maybe it won't be so bad," Nina said thoughtfully.

"Oh, no? Even my best friend suddenly has a new guy interested in her. *They're* going to the Christmas dance." Kelly slumped in the chair, totally dejected. "Nina, it's more than just being alone. I was really counting on these two weeks of vacation to be together with Eric. I was going to make up for all the time I've been busy with modeling. Now I won't have that, and by the time he comes back, I'll be busy with work again."

Nina's face softened in sympathy. "That *is* too bad."

"I don't know how I'll ever live through this vacation. Listen, Nina, I really do want to work. Dog food ads, anything. Just please, please get me some jobs!"

Nina's eyes began to sparkle. "Not dog food ads," she said with a smile. "I'll try to come up with something a little better than that."

"I don't care what it is." With one more sigh, Kelly gathered her things together and stood up to go. Without looking back, she headed for the front door. "Well, Merry Christmas, everyone," she called halfheartedly.

Nobody looking at Kelly's face would ever have guessed that it was Christmas Eve. Her pretty features seemed to be in a permanent expression of gloom, the complete opposite of all the bright, cheerful photographs where she was posed grinning from ear to ear and looking as though she hadn't a care in the world.

Kelly's mother was baking pies. She looked at Kelly, who was sitting at the kitchen table and drawing patterns in some spilled sugar, and sighed. "It isn't the end of the world, Kelly!"

"Yes, it is." The Powerses had just left for the airport. Kelly had watched their car pull away from their white-shingled house right across the street.

The doorbell rang, and Kelly stood up listlessly. "I'll get it." She walked slowly to the door and opened it.

"Hi, stranger—can I come in?" Her best friend, Jennifer Lee, was standing on the doorstep, her dark eyes sparkling.

"Jen! What are you doing here?" Kelly asked.

"I came to give you your Christmas present. I meant to bring it sooner, but"—she ducked her head—"the time seems to be going so fast. This vacation will be over before we know it!"

"Going fast? This day's been dragging on forever!"

Jen nodded sympathetically. "I guess it seems long to you. I mean, because you're probably missing Eric already."

"They just left. At least he came over this morning to say good-bye. Oh, well . . . come on up to my room."

Jennifer followed her upstairs. "Look, Kelly, I know I haven't been around much the last few days, but it's not that I'm trying to avoid you."

"You're just busy, huh?"

"Yeah, I mean, Kip is amazing—he always has

something to do. He asked me to the movies night before last, and then last night he called up to ask me out for pizza. It's like a dream or something. But you know how it is, I mean, you've gone out with movie stars and all. You're used to people fussing over you."

"Yeah, I suppose so. But it's not so strange, Jen. By the time you noticed Kip, he was already crazy about you. The date for the dance just set everything in motion." Kelly sat down at her desk and looked out the window.

When Kelly turned around, she saw Jennifer place a beautiful, silver-wrapped box on the bed. "Here's your present," Jennifer said quietly. "I hope you like it."

Kelly reached under the desk to pick up an unwrapped gift box. She felt herself flush, and suddenly she felt guilty for her lack of energy. "Uh, this is yours. I didn't have much luck with the wrapping. If you wait a minute, I'll fix it."

"That's okay, it's fine, really."

"No, Jen, please wait." Kelly took the box back from Jennifer and sat on the edge of the bed with some wrapping paper and a pair of scissors. "I'm sorry. I don't mean to take it out on you, but I've felt so lousy all week. First Eric lets me down, then you've been so busy. I guess I feel kind of left out."

"That's rough," Jennifer agreed. "Especially when you had such great plans for this vacation."

Kelly forced a smile. "So . . . tell me what you're wearing to the Christmas dance." The telephone rang, but she decided to let her mother get it downstairs. *It couldn't possibly be for me,* she thought.

"Mom and I decided the dress would be her big present to me," Jennifer said. "We picked it out over the weekend. It—"

"Kelly!" Mrs. Blake called. "Telephone. It's Meg."

"I'd better go," Jennifer said.

"Wait a minute!" Kelly cried. "We haven't opened our presents yet. Unless you're in a big hurry. This can't be anything important."

"No, I can wait." Jennifer sat back as Kelly picked up the phone in her room.

"Hello?"

"Kelly—marvelous news," Meg said. "I was afraid you'd be off on one of those school events you've been talking about."

Kelly tried to sound blasé. "It turns out nothing much is happening after all."

"No? Well, all the more reason to put you back to work. It's a good thing I had you get a passport when you started working for me. This assignment is for Bonjour cosmetics. You'll have to fly to Paris for a week, but you told Nina you'd take anything. In fact, this was Nina's idea. When the model we'd lined up was rejected at the last minute, Nina insisted you'd be right for the job."

For a minute, Kelly couldn't even speak. When she could talk again, her voice came out in a squeak. "Paris? Paris! Oh, Meg—when do I go? Are you serious?"

"The day after Christmas. You'll barely have time to pack. I'll have to speak to your mother. She'll go with you, of course. That won't be a problem, will it?"

"Are you kidding? My mother has never been to Paris—she'll love it. And she has a passport, too! My parents went to London for their tenth anniversary." She was babbling, she knew. *Paris! Eric! Oh, thank you, Nina,* she thought fervently.

"What about leaving your sister behind?"

"My dad can handle it. Besides, Tina is old enough to take care of herself. Or she can stay with a friend. She's no problem."

"Fine. That's what I like to hear. This is all very last-minute, so you have to be certain you get all the information straight. I've already booked seats on the six forty-five out of Kennedy International Airport for you and your mother. Now make sure you bring these things with you . . ."

Kelly only half listened to what Meg was saying. Her head was swimming. Not only was she working, she was working for a famous cosmetics company, one of the best accounts in the agency! And in Paris! With Eric!

Suddenly a fear pricked her joy. *What if Eric doesn't want to see me there? He has his itinerary all planned out. What if our relationship can't make it away from home, away from school and our friends? We've had so many problems with my breaking dates for my modeling. . . .*

". . . and electrical converters, if you have them," Meg finished.

"What? Oh, sure, Meg. Listen, I'll put my mom on the phone and you can explain everything to her. I've got to start packing!"

Jennifer could hardly believe her ears. "Paris! You and your mom? I don't believe it."

Kelly threw jeans and skirts and blouses onto the bed. "I can't wait. Talk about a dream come true!"

"You lead a charmed life," Jennifer marveled. "What incredible luck! Wait until Eric finds out you're there. You can call him before you leave. Oh! You do have his number in Paris, don't you?"

Kelly frowned. "We're looking after their house, so they left the number in case anything came up. But I'd better wait and call him when I get there. It's expensive to call Paris."

"Kelly! I'm sure your parents won't mind. This is important."

"Well . . . there *is* something else. I wasn't exactly a ball of fire when I said good-bye to him today. He had his whole vacation planned, every place he wanted to go, everything he wanted to see. What if he couldn't wait to get away without me?"

Jennifer made a face. "You don't believe that, not for one minute. Eric is crazy about you. Things will be completely different once you're really in Paris."

Kelly continued to pack, a worried look on her face. "I hope so, Jen," she said.

Two

The day after Christmas, the Blake household was in utter chaos. Jennifer knew that things were topsy-turvy the minute she stepped in the door. Empty suitcases were scattered all over the hall, and Kelly and Tina and Mrs. Blake were all talking at once.

"Here I am," Jennifer announced, with her biggest smile. "Just tell me what to do and I'll do it."

"Everything," Kelly yelled, exasperated. "My dad will be here soon and nobody's even packed! I'm not nearly ready."

"You're not the only one getting ready," Mrs.

Blake told her sharply. "Tina has to get packed too. Ivy and her mother will be here any minute."

"Tina is going around the corner to her best friend's house," Kelly complained. "*I* am going to Europe."

"I don't want to go to Ivy's," Tina said crankily. "I told you, I don't feel well."

Kelly rolled her eyes. "This has been going on all day. Tina, I think you're just jealous."

"I'm not jealous," Tina insisted, "I'm sick."

"Then you shouldn't have stuffed yourself at Christmas dinner yesterday. And you ate all that fruitcake this morning, instead of breakfast. Yech, no wonder you feel sick."

"You ate just as much as me," Tina said.

"Girls, that's enough!" Mrs. Blake put her hands over her ears. "Tina, come here, please." She took a close look at her younger daughter. "You do look awfully flushed, honey." She put her hand on Tina's forehead and exclaimed, "Why, you're burning up!"

"I don't believe it." Kelly put her hand on Tina's forehead also. She pulled it away. "She *is* hot," she said, shocked.

Ten minutes later, Tina was in pajamas and tucked into bed. Mrs. Blake closed the door to her room softly, shaking her head in a worried way. "Everyone's been so keyed up—I thought she was just overexcited. But her temperature is very high."

Kelly was completely frazzled. "Mom, we've got to get ready! Dad will be here soon—we can't miss this flight, there's only one a day to Paris."

"It's out of the question, sweetheart," Mrs. Blake said calmly. "I'm not going anywhere. Not with Tina so sick."

Kelly swallowed hard. "What are you talking about? You have go to—Mom, please, this is very important to me."

"Kelly, I'm sorry. I can't leave Tina like this. And she certainly can't stay with Ivy, or with anyone else."

"But Dad can take care of her."

"Not when he's working, he can't. She has a temperature of one hundred and four. She needs attention. I wouldn't leave you, Kelly, and you know it."

"But, Mom, this is the Bonjour account. Everything's all arranged and it's too late to get another model now. Meg will kill me. I'll never work again!"

"Well, you're not going to Europe alone, and that's final," Mrs. Blake said firmly.

"You're not being fair," Kelly cried. "Why does everything happen to me? This is a total disaster."

"Call Meg," Jennifer suggested. "She'll know what to do."

Kelly ran to the telephone in the kitchen and

called the FLASH! number. "Please be there, Meg," she prayed, crossing her fingers. "Please, please be there!"

Meg was in. Frantically, Kelly explained what was happening.

"First of all, take it easy," Meg told her. "No way are we going to cancel this booking. It's far too important. We'll just have to make other arrangements. Let me think for a moment."

"Meg says I'm going," Kelly told her mother triumphantly.

"We'll see about that," Mrs. Blake answered, taking the phone away from her.

Kelly listened anxiously, trying to tell what was happening from her mother's responses and expression. Finally, Mrs. Blake hung up the phone. "Well? Tell me what Meg said," Kelly begged. "What's going on?"

Mrs. Blake took a deep breath. "Well, Meg convinced me that this trip is absolutely necessary."

"Yippee," Kelly and Jennifer screamed at once.

"Shhh—Tina's sleeping," Mrs. Blake reminded them. "Meg said she would call a woman named Simone—she's the FLASH! agent in Paris. Meg will arrange for Simone to meet you at the airport and take you to your hotel and to the photography studio. Simone is about fifty, with salt-and-pepper hair like Meg's, and she's seen your pictures, of course, so you shouldn't have any trouble finding each other. In any event, Meg gave me Simone's home and office phone numbers. Meg assures me there'll be no slip-up, but, write the numbers down just in case."

"It's not going to be very much fun," Kelly complained. "This Simone probably won't let me do anything. Mom and I were going to go sightseeing in my free time," she said to Jennifer. "Now I'll be in Paris, France, and I won't be able to go anywhere!"

"Meg and I thought of that, too," her mother assured her. "You're forgetting one thing—the Powers family is in Paris, and Ellen did leave me their number in case of an emergency. I'd say this is an emergency. You can go sight-seeing with Eric and his family—I know you'll like that. I'll call Paris right now and make sure Ellen Powers knows where to get in touch with you and this Simone. I'll feel a lot better knowing the Powerses are there too. I don't quite trust a total stranger, no matter what Meg says. Ellen is a good friend, she'll make sure you're taken care of."

Kelly stared at her mother as she went to make the phone call.

"This is working out great," Jennifer whispered excitedly. "You'll be able to hang out with Eric the whole time. Don't you see? It couldn't have worked out any better."

Kelly began to feel more hopeful. "Jen . . . why are you always right?" she asked and gave her friend a grateful hug.

The flight attendant announced the time as 8:00 A.M. when the huge Air France Boeing 747 touched down in France at Charles de Gaulle Airport. The sky looked gray and dismal, but it couldn't quench Kelly's mood: Christmas week in Paris, the city of lights, the most romantic place in the world!

Kelly glanced at her watch. Two o'clock. It was still the middle of the night back home. As she reset her watch to Paris time, she thought of her parents, her sister Tina, and Jennifer. They would all be fast asleep right now, and here she was already starting a new day. And without any sleep! She'd been too excited to really sleep on the flight. Now a sudden awareness of her own fatigue swept over her. But she tossed her hair over her shoulder as if to sweep it away. Maybe her body still thought it was in New Jersey, but her mind knew she was in Paris, and she wanted to be awake enough to enjoy it. Tomorrow she would start her assignment with the Bonjour people. "Rest up the day you get there," Meg had advised her. "I don't want you to look all jet-lagged on the Bonjour ads. And don't forget you're there to work," Meg had warned. "The Bonjour people wouldn't take too kindly to the idea that they're sponsoring a neighborhood get-together."

"Oh, Meg!" she'd protested. "I don't even know if the Powers family will have any time for me." Meg had only laughed. She expected a lot from her models, but she gave a lot back too.

The flight attendant, a blond woman named Irene, noticed Kelly struggling to remove her carry-on luggage from under the seat in front of her. She bent down and easily slid the bag out.

"Thanks," Kelly told her. "You've been really helpful. Everyone has."

As she filed off the plane with the other first-class passengers, Kelly's head felt muffled and fuzzy from her lack of sleep. Her stomach growled, not from hunger but from excitement and nervousness. Now that she was finally in Paris, she felt terribly young and completely unsure of herself. Why had she ever told Meg she could handle this trip alone? Seven days in a strange country—anything could happen.

The exit ramp opened into the busy airport terminal, and Kelly's thoughts quickly returned to her immediate surroundings. Her father, ever the policeman, had warned her to be especially careful in the airport, but all Kelly saw were holiday travelers, airport shops done up in colorful decorations, and stand-up cafés where people were waiting for their flights to board. All around her, people were, like her, on their way to work or to visit family, and the excitement of the Christmas holiday was in the air.

Mr. Blake had explained to Kelly the procedures for collecting her bags and passing through Passport Control and Customs. She felt as if she were in a dream as she went through the motions. Free at last, she scanned the terminal for any sign of Simone. A tiny knot of fear formed in her stomach. What if she didn't find her?

A figure suddenly blocked her view.

"Eric!" She stared at him, her mind spinning.

"Hi, Kelly!" Eric said with a sheepish grin. "Your mom called and told us all about your job here, and she said a FLASH! agent named Simone was going to meet you at the airport."

"Then what are you doing here?" Kelly was torn between joy and confusion.

"Well, my mom called Simone right away, but there was no answer. She tried half the night and again this morning, and all she got was an answering service. They swore Simone had been given the message and would be here to meet you, but you know my mother—she doesn't trust strangers. So this morning she left a message saying we'd meet you instead."

"She's just like my mother." Kelly sighed and

yawned and smiled in rapid succession, and Eric frowned in concern.

"Are you all right? Do you feel okay?" He pried her fingers away from her carry-on bag and cradled her hand in his.

"Yes, I'm fine! Just a little tired. But—oh, Eric! I couldn't exchange any money at home because of the holiday. Meg said that was okay, Simone would give me an allowance here. I don't have any francs—just some American cash that Mom and Dad gave me!"

"That's okay," Eric said. "Come on, I'll take you to a bank right here and you can exchange your money for francs."

Kelly was grateful for Eric's help as she completed the transaction. Then they went outside the terminal.

Eric had taken over Kelly's blue suitcase, which held casual clothes—shirts, jeans, sweaters, sneakers—and her slim pink bag. That one held two dresses, scarves, a leather skirt, and a pair of black boots. Not the stuff Kelly usually wore, but she wanted to look her best in Paris. She had her carry-on, and the small red bag that held her makeup—lipsticks, frosty blushes, pearlized eye shadows, fat black eye-pencils, and moisturizing creams. Nina had said the Bonjour people would be using their own makeup, but Kelly had decided to bring her own, anyway.

Another job might suddenly come in. Or a last-minute date at a Parisian nightspot.

Kelly eyed Eric's new silk scarf as they approached a cab in the taxi line. He seemed to be enjoying Paris! Struggling with his French, Eric explained their destination. The driver nodded, and put Kelly's luggage into the trunk as she and Eric slid into the backseat. Kelly glanced at Eric beside her, then stared out the window into the late December grayness. It didn't look quite so dismal now.

She put her head back as another wave of fatigue washed over her. She couldn't seem to keep her eyes open.

"Put your head on my shoulder," Eric suggested. Kelly did, and when she awoke, they were in Paris, the city of love.

"This is some place," Eric whispered to Kelly as they followed a bellboy along a long corridor.

Before Kelly could answer, the bellboy put down her bags and swung open a door. She stepped past him.

"Oh, Eric! Isn't it beautiful!" Kelly's jet lag faded as she looked around the room. She'd been in luxury hotel rooms before, but nothing like this! A huge four-poster bed stood in the middle of the large, airy room. Two floor-to-ceiling windows looked out over the Champs-Elysées, while two more showed a magnificent view of the Arc de Triomphe.

"Hey—isn't that the Eiffel Tower?" Eric called. But Kelly had already wandered into the bathroom. There, against beautifully patterned pink wallpaper, stood the biggest bathtub she'd ever seen! Unlike tubs in the States, it had no shower. On the opposite wall, a sink stood in a marble stand, with faucets that looked like real gold.

"Kelly?" Eric stopped at the door of the bathroom. Then he, too, stared at the tub. "Wow! I hope you brought your swimsuit. You could do laps in that thing!"

Kelly laughed. "I'm too tired for laps right now, but I wouldn't mind lots of bubbles and a good soak."

The bellboy coughed gently, and Kelly and Eric both turned around quickly. They'd forgotten he was still here. Kelly hesitated, not knowing how much to tip him. But Eric pulled some change out of his pocket. *"Merci,"* he said.

The bellboy smiled. Then his attention was caught by something across the room. *"Mademoiselle. Regardez."* He pointed to the telephone.

Kelly noticed that the red light was flashing. She had a message! "Oh, thank you," she said. *"Merci."* The bellboy smiled again and left.

"Just a sec, Eric." Kelly sat on the bed and called the message desk. "It's from Simone!" she announced to Eric, covering the phone. She listened to the operator, mentally translating the French. Could she have heard correctly? Simone seemed awfully brusque from her message.

She turned to Eric. "Simone received the message that you'd meet me, and she'll see me at six tomorrow evening at the studio. Then she left the address. No welcome to Paris or anything!"

"She'll see you at *six?*"

"Yes, I'll be working evenings for the most part. The job is for a cosmetics company, but they're going to photograph me in all sorts of designer fashions, Meg said. Because it's the Christmas season, the clothes are needed in the boutiques during the day. You see, the dresses are one of a kind, and a lot of customers come in from all over the world to see them at this time of year. Bonjour can only borrow them at night. So we work from six to midnight." Kelly yawned again.

"I hope I'll still get to see you!" Eric said. "In fact, I thought I'd take you out for a walk now if you're not too tired. There's so much for you to see."

So Eric *was* glad she was there! Kelly remembered Meg's instructions to get plenty of rest, but

Eric's face was so eager she couldn't resist him. *Just one quick walk—then I'll take a nap*, she decided.

"Hold on," she told him, smiling. "I'll change and be out in a sec." She took a suitcase into the bathroom and closed the door. A few minutes later, she appeared in black stirrup pants and a long red-and-black-checked sweater. Eric looked at her approvingly and then grabbed her hand. "Let's go!"

In the hotel elevator, Kelly pretended to snooze on Eric's shoulder, but her excitement at seeing Paris was beginning to perk her up. Outside, the streets were alive with activity. It was two days after Christmas, yet people seemed to be shopping as if the holiday were fast approaching. When Kelly pointed this out to Eric, he explained that Parisians shopped in a different manner than Americans.

"They're really just window-shopping," he explained. "French shopkeepers seem to display most of their wares in the windows, so customers don't enter a shop unless they have something specific to buy."

Kelly studied Eric's face. "How did you learn so much about this place so quickly?"

"Well, I've been here three days already," he said. "And I've picked up a lot from my aunt Cecile."

"Eric—look at the cars! They're so small! And fast!"

"The French do drive fast, but they're pretty good drivers," Eric told her. "Just don't make the mistake of jaywalking. Drivers have the right of way here."

"Drivers have the right of way?" The idea seemed bizarre to Kelly.

"Sounds weird, I know," Eric said. "But back home drivers *act* as if they have the right of way, anyway, so maybe it works out better here. Puts pedestrians on their guard, at least. And speaking of home, what's happening there?" Eric asked, taking her hand in his as they walked along. "Is everyone ready for the dance?"

Kelly laughed. "You should hear Jennifer. You'd think she just invented boys, she's so excited about going to the dance with Kip." She looked at Eric's face. His eyes were on her, studying her. She felt odd—slightly uncomfortable, yet strangely pleased. It was fun being in a strange place; everything you said or did seemed to have special meaning.

"Hey, I just remembered something," Eric said. "I promised to pick up some sort of hand cream for my mom. Maybe you can help me out?"

"Sure thing. Are we going to a drugstore?"

"Not exactly. Drugstores here are called pharmacies. They're more oriented toward medicine. Aunt Cecile suggested I go to a five-and-ten."

"A French five-and-ten!" Kelly snuggled closer to Eric. "That sounds like fun!"

"As much fun as walking with me?" Eric asked, teasing.

The five-and-ten turned out to be a large store on the Champs-Elysées. Kelly noticed that the merchandise on display—silk scarves, belts, bags, and costume jewelry—could only be found in larger department stores back home.

They quickly found the hand cream Eric's mother wanted. As Eric carefully counted out the French money to pay for his purchase, Kelly spied a makeup counter two aisles away. "Eric! I'll meet you over there—by the makeup, okay?" Kelly said and dashed off.

The colors and variety of makeup on display almost made Kelly gasp: the counter resembled a huge, bright, child's paint box. There were rows of eye shadows in colors so vivid that Kelly wanted every single one. And pencils . . . rows and rows of them, displayed like artists' colors. And lipsticks . . . She just had to try some of the colors on her hand. Frosty pink . . . hot orange . . . scarlet red—even white, pearly blue, and black! She felt dazzled by the choices. "No wonder the Bonjour account is so big!" she said when Eric joined her. "The French are serious about their cosmetics. Look at this black lipstick. I wonder how I'd look wearing that?"

"Not like Kelly Blake, that's for sure. Listen, Kelly. My parents invited you over today. I thought you might want to nap this afternoon, but I can come get you later, if you want to have dinner with us."

"That's fine. And I'd like a nap, but only a short one," Kelly added. She didn't want to miss a second of being with Eric.

"Great!" Eric took her hand in his and led her down a narrow side street. Kelly wondered why they'd left the broad boulevard, but she really didn't care. As long as she was with Eric, all the streets of Paris were beautiful.

"Here we are," Eric said, stopping in front of a small restaurant. "It doesn't look like much, I know." He smiled at the expression on Kelly's face. "It's a bistro—sort of a workers' restaurant—but my uncle Didier told me the food's great. It's not fancy, but it's really French—and real French people eat here, too, not tourists."

"Oh, Eric, I love it! I—I feel like a real Parisian."

When they left the bistro two hours later, Kelly felt she knew why Paris was called the city of love. Everything was so romantic, even the workers' restaurants.

"Well," Eric said, "I guess it's time to get you back to your hotel." He kissed her lightly. "And maybe I'll come up and tuck you in."

"Eric—you will not!"

"Not *this* time," he teased.

Kelly looped her arm through his, the way she'd noticed a French girl walk with her boyfriend. So far, this trip was the best thing that had ever happened to her.

Three

Kelly's nap and a luxurious soak in the gigantic bathtub refreshed her, and apparently it showed. When Eric's parents first saw her, they both exclaimed over how well she looked. His younger brother, Timmy, said "Hi," and asked if she was as hungry as he was. And Eric just grinned at her.

The restaurant they dined in was small but distinctive. Faded red velvet covered the walls, but they were so thickly hung with old photographs and drawings in gilt-edged frames that the velvet could barely be seen. The decor fascinated Timmy so much that he talked about nothing else all through dinner. Kelly, Eric, and his parents talked about the delicious food.

"I have to thank you, Mr. and Mrs. Powers," Kelly said as she slid her chair out from the table. "I've never had a meal like that in my life!"

"It was good, wasn't it," Eric's father said proudly. "Tourists don't know about this place. Cecile and Didier let us in on a well-kept secret."

"Cecile has become so European," Mrs. Powers added. "I can barely recognize the baby sister who used to follow me everywhere. You'll get a chance to meet her tomorrow, Kelly—you're invited to their apartment for lunch."

Eric grinned at Kelly and took her hand under the table. "I knew Mom would try to take over your life."

"I don't mind," she protested politely. "I hate to eat alone."

"You see, Eric—I told you she'd be pleased." Mrs. Powers beamed at Kelly.

Eric cleared his throat loudly.

"Don't worry"—Mr. Powers winked at his son—"you'll have plenty of time together."

Kelly hoped this was true. Actually she was hoping to have plenty of time *alone* with Eric.

When their cab pulled up outside Kelly's hotel, she was very happy to hear Mr. Powers say, "We'll wait out here for you, Eric. Not too long."

Eric kissed her good night at the elevators—a quick kiss. "Tomorrow," he whispered. "Tomorrow, after lunch, we'll make up for lost time."

* * *

Eric's mother was right when she said her sister Cecile has become completely French, thought Kelly as she sipped coffee after lunch in Madame des Barres's charming dining room. When Kelly and Eric first arrived at the handsome nineteenth-century apartment building near the Bois de Vincennes, Cecile had served them sparkling water while the adults drank aperitifs. After that, they'd had crudités, or raw vegetables, and then hors d'oeuvres, a huge platter of pâtés and a variety of seafoods. The main course had been steak with fried potatoes and string beans, followed by a huge, fresh salad, then cheese. After that, fruit and pastry had been served. When, finally, coffee was poured, Kelly thought she would burst.

She glanced over at Eric and thought he looked fidgety. Certainly neither of them had sat at such a lengthy meal before! It was a far cry from the fast foods they ate in the States. And even though the meal was delicious, it seemed somehow a waste to spend four daylight hours eating lunch—especially when she and Eric might have spent the time together exploring Paris on their own. *Perhaps there's still time*, Kelly thought. Eric's uncle had insisted on driving her to the photography studio, but if it was still early enough, he might agree to just drop them in the center of town. Eric could take the Metro or a bus back. She glanced at her watch.

Didier des Barres saw her and smiled. "Are you ready to go, Kelly? Eric? We must allow for the heavier traffic at this time of day."

Even though she was disappointed, Kelly had to smile at the way Didier said his nephew's name—*Ereec*, pronoucing the *i* like an *e* and stresssing the second syllable instead of the first. As she stood up to leave, she caught Eric's eye. He looked as glum as she felt. Perhaps he, too, had been thinking about how they might have spent the afternoon. She glanced around. The others had moved toward the hall—they were practically alone! She took Eric's hand. "Come, Ereec," she murmured in a heavy French accent. "Come weet me to ze 'art of Paree."

Eric laughed, and they left the room hand in hand.

When they reached the photography studio, Eric's uncle waited in the car while Eric took Kelly inside.

The elevator doors opened onto a sleek, modern hallway. A sign on the wall in front of them read VILLANOVA STUDIO.

Kelly knocked on the frosted glass of the door. A fiftyish, salt-and-pepper-haired woman opened it abruptly. "You are Kelly Blake, I suppose. I am Simone." She said her name as if she were announcing a royal title. "You are lucky—you are on time for your first day of work."

"I'm lucky?" Kelly stared at Simone. "I know how to get to work on time."

Simone clucked her tongue and glared at Eric. "And who are you? Do not answer, it really does not matter." She turned back to Kelly, furious. "Did Meg not tell you? No boys. Not when you are working for me. You are only sixteen. No boys at all, understand?"

Kelly's mouth dropped open. Eric tried to explain. "I happen to be a friend of the family's," he began, but Simone cut him short, grabbing Kelly's arm and leading her through the studio doorway. "Enough! I hope I do not see you up here again—understood?" Eric gave her a cold stare, then turned on his heel and headed for the elevators.

Kelly was boiling mad. "How dare you . . ." she sputtered.

Simone ignored her words and led her through a long hallway that finally opened into a wide, spacious studio. A tall, dark man wearing a white wool turtleneck hurried to greet them.

"This is the only man in your life for as long as you are here," Simone declared. "Patrick Villanova."

"Ah, *bonsoir*!" he greeted her. "I love American models. They are always on time, exactly on time. Did you get some rest from your trip?"

"I'm fine," Kelly said, although she was starting to feel quite tired.

"Simone, my love," Patrick said to the older woman, "thank you for delivering Kelly. Now let us get to work." He dismissed her with a wave of his hand, and to Kelly's surprise, Simone went without a word.

"I don't understand that woman," Kelly began. "She's impossible . . ."

Patrick smiled widely at her, his white teeth flashing against his dark beard and mustache. "Forget about Simone. You are my model, and I have heard all about you."

"Oh?" Kelly didn't know quite what to do. Thank him? His remark made it sound as if he thought he owned her.

"Well, make yourself at home in the dressing room." Patrick took her coat and hung it near the door. "If you are hungry I can order up some food."

"Oh, I'm not hungry at all," Kelly said hastily.

Before long, the entire cast had arrived. There was a cute strawberry-blond British model named Bonnie Cooper, and a striking Swedish girl named Inge Lindstrom. Several women and a male art director were there from Bonjour, and there was a short, jolly little man who said he was Tristan, the hair and makeup artist. The last person to arrive was a very pretty model from the French division of FLASH! named simply

Nathalie. Kelly thought she looked slightly familiar—had she worked in the States?

"Excuse me"—Kelly held a hand out to the girl—"you look very familiar. Have we met?"

Nathalie stared rudely at Kelly, ignoring her hand. "I doubt that," she said sharply. She had a thick French accent, but seemed very sure of her English. Kelly tried again.

"Have you ever been in the United States? You seem to speak English very . . ."

"Please." Nathalie cut her off. "You Americans are so rude. You speak no French, but think all the French should know your language. I've heard it all before. Just please, leave me alone."

Kelly drew back, stung. She wanted to point out that she was taking third-year French, but a slight tug at her arm indicated that Tristan had spread his wares out on the dressing room counter and was ready to make her up for the photographic shoot. Kelly sat on a swivel chair and tied a yellow scarf around her head to keep her hair out of her face. Tristan began by rubbing base foundation into her skin. He used swirling motions with his fingers to spread the makeup onto her face, massaging her neck and throat to get as even a color as possible. Having her foundation done was almost Kelly's favorite part of modeling. And every time, she had the same thought: *Imagine getting paid while someone gives you a relaxing facial massage!* As Tristan

applied contour powder and blush with light, soft
strokes, using brushes held in either hand, Kelly
felt so relaxed she thought she might fall asleep.
Her lids felt as though they were weighted down
with tiny sandbags. The chatter of the other
models around her began to recede. As Tristan
applied translucent powder with a huge, soft
brush, Kelly fell fast asleep.

She was roused out of sleep moments later by a
hand shaking her shoulder. "Hey, wake up! *Mon
Dieu!*" Nathalie, the French model, stood over
her. "I have to get my makeup done. Would you
mind sleeping somewhere else?"

Kelly, feeling very groggy, only stared. What
right did Nathalie have to be so rude, so nasty?

Tristan chuckled. "Hold on, Nathalie. Let her
catch up on her sleep if she needs it."

Gratefully, Kelly got up slowly. Bonnie gave
her a sympathetic smile. "It's a bit rough, isn't
it?" she said. "I know the feeling. I've flown to
the United States on assignment a few times, but
jet lag seems to be the most severe coming this
way."

Inge nodded her head and said, "*Ja,*" in
agreement. Kelly smiled at them, glad that at
least these two girls would be good company
during the long nights ahead. Nathalie certainly
wouldn't be—she seemed selfish and self-
absorbed. *It'll be a shame*, Kelly thought, if *one
girl spoils the whole shoot.*

She peeked out of the dressing room. Patrick had put on some American rock music, a little too loudly, to wake everyone up. He sat drinking coffee with the representatives from Bonjour, going over layouts of the shots they had in mind for the evening. The art director explained everything, gesturing with his hand and waving a cigarette around wildly. Presently, there was a knock at the studio door and the first of the evening's garments arrived. Patrick carried a couple of them to the dressing room where the models were waiting and hung them up.

Nathalie's eyes brightened when Patrick entered the room. "Have you seen my latest film?" she asked Patrick. Kelly noticed she used a different tone of voice toward Patrick than she did in speaking to the models.

"Of course!" Patrick winked at the dark girl. "It was marvelous."

"What are they talking about?" Bonnie whispered.

"Oh, Nathalie's bragging about her movie again," Inge told her matter-of-factly. "As if she's a big star—she's been in two films and she was only on screen about one minute altogether."

"You'd think she was famous, the way she treats the rest of us." Bonnie glared toward Nathalie. "She thinks she's quite a big shot and the rest of us are just lowly models."

Kelly watched as Nathalie held her head back,

eyes closed, while Tristan applied the finishing touches to her makeup. So Nathalie was an aspiring actress. Perhaps that was where Kelly had seen her before. "I've seen a couple of French films in New York," she told Inge. "Maybe Nathalie was in one of them."

"I doubt that. Her biggest roles are in her imagination," Inge said with a smile.

"Okay, next," Tristan announced. Nathalie got up to admire the fashions that Patrick had brought in, and Bonnie sat down at the makeup table. Nathalie lifted a flowing deep rose dress off the rack. "Oh, it's beautiful!" she breathed. "Patrick, *chéri*," she called out, "are you ready for the first shot? I've got my dress all picked out."

"Darling!" Patrick stepped into the dressing room. "That would look stunning on you, but Kelly's going to start in that one."

Nathalie's eyes flashed at Kelly. "But why?" Nathalie pouted. "What difference does it make who wears what? Do you honestly think that little American is going to make the dress look better than I could?"

Inge rolled her eyes toward Kelly, while Bonnie looked as insulted as if Nathalie were talking about her.

"Natie, Natie!" Patrick put on a paternal air. "The people from Bonjour have already decided.

They want Kelly to wear the dress. Don't worry, darling, the best are yet to come!"

Pouting, but soothed, Nathalie sat down at the counter, rearranging the hairdo Tristan had just created. He nearly misapplied a stroke of lipstick to Bonnie's upturned mouth. "Honey, please," he pleaded. "My best hairdo of the evening. You wouldn't spoil it now, would you?"

"Of course not," Nathalie answered. "I'm making it better." Behind her back, Inge and Bonnie made faces at each other. It was clear to Kelly that they already disliked Nathalie. How would they all get through the rest of the week with things so tense when the job hadn't even started yet? Plus, Kelly's jet lag was really beginning to overwhelm her. She wondered how she was going to make it through the evening.

Just then, one of the Bonjour executives entered the dressing room. "Is the first girl ready?" she asked. "Come on, Kelly. Put that deep rose dress on. We're waiting for you: *vite alors!*"

Kelly jumped out of her knit dress and folded it over the back of a chair. The dressing room was in total chaos. Kelly waded through a pile of shoes and boots and bags on the floor to get to the rose-colored dress. As she slipped the dress over her head, Kelly could feel Nathalie's eyes on her, measuring and judging, probably hoping that the dress wouldn't fit. But it did, of course. Kelly was a true size eight, and most designer's samples fit her perfectly. Meg had said she had one of the best bodies in the business.

The dress was a soft, filmy evening gown. A sheer panel draped over one shoulder, spilling onto the floor like a train. The deep rose color flattered Kelly's vibrant coloring, and she knew without looking in the mirror that she was at her absolute best in the gown. Suddenly she didn't feel at all tired, and she couldn't resist a triumphant glance at Nathalie.

"I still say I would look much better than you in it," Nathalie announced brazenly. "Your hair is on the dark side, but mine is black. It is much more striking with that dress color. Anyone would prefer to see me in the dress than you."

"Then why aren't you wearing it?" Kelly asked stiffly.

Nathalie shrugged. "Perhaps Patrick thinks he likes you better. American girls have the reputation for being—easy, that is how you say it, no?"

Nathalie's insults were just too much! Kelly had to bite her lip to keep from blurting out what she really wanted to say. Clearly, Nathalie couldn't get along with other models. Kelly had met the type before, girls too jealous and scared of competition to ever make friends. She almost felt sorry for Nathalie.

"Good." The Bonjour executive approved, handing Kelly a pair of lace gloves that reached the elbow. Tristan stopped doing Bonnie's make-

up to fasten a little white cap on Kelly's head.
When that was done, he added a pink frost to her
lips. Kelly caught a glimpse of herself in the
mirror.

There was no way anybody could tell she had
jet lag—she looked stunning! She caught another
glance from Nathalie, but pretended not to
notice. After Tristan added a last touch of pearly
blush to her cheeks, she stepped out into the
studio where Patrick and the others were waiting
for her. "Sensational!" Patrick cried.

The Bonjour executives immediately began
talking among themselves. Their French was too
fast for Kelly, but she could tell that they were
pleased. A red-haired woman balanced a cigarette in her mouth while she bent to pull at
Kelly's hemline. A man rearranged the pearls at
her neck. No one seemed to notice that she was a
living, breathing person and not just a store-
window mannequin.

Only Patrick seemed aware that she was a
person, and even he went on and on about
"discovering her," and weren't the Bonjour people happy that he'd managed to get her to Paris
after all? Kelly almost laughed aloud. She knew
Nina had made the recommendation to Patrick.

Still, she thought it best to humor Patrick.
Fashion photographers were famous for their
lines. They wanted to believe that while you
worked for them, you were attracted to them.

Meg had warned her about it. "Just pretend to go along with it," she'd said. "But when it's time to go home, head straight for the door." Kelly smiled at Patrick politely.

"Are you ready for me on the set?" she asked.

"*Oui, oui.*" Patrick motioned to his assistant. "Fabian! A light-reading, please."

Kelly went to the far end of the studio, where Patrick had prepared a backdrop of white paper. Several light sources bathed the paper in a variety of pastel colors. The final effect was surprisingly beautiful.

Fabian held a light meter to her face while Patrick tested his flash. "Four-nine. Four-three," Fabian said, calling off the readings. When they were what Patrick expected, he nodded approvingly. When they were off, he scowled impatiently, and Fabian adjusted the lights for another reading. Finally Patrick was satisfied with the results. The Bonjour people gave one last tug at Kelly's dress, pulled the earrings off her ears in exchange for another pair, and finally, she was ready.

Patrick nodded at Kelly approvingly. "Okay, *chérie*. Here is the feeling we want to have. This ad is for makeup, as you know. You are the most beautiful girl in the world. You are the Bonjour girl. You wear the best makeup in the world. And you are wearing the best fashions in the world." He turned to the red-haired woman. "Who is the creator of this fabulous dress?"

"Amalfi," she said matter-of-factly.

"Ah, Amalfi." Patrick turned back to Kelly, ecstasy on his face. "My dear—you are wearing an Amalfi original. You are the first girl to wear it. All others are envying you."

Kelly thought of Nathalie back in the dressing room. She certainly envied her this dress!

"Don't let your mind wander!" Patrick shouted. "We almost had the mood right. Let's try again. You are the chosen one, the most beautiful, the most original. Ah—that's it. Hold it!"

As Kelly held her expression, Patrick snapped a Polaroid. "*Bon*," he told her. "Now relax, and let's see how the Polaroid comes out."

A minute later, Fabian had torn open the Polaroid, and he and Patrick made a few last-minute adjustments to the lights. Then they were ready to begin. Kelly's earrings were changed one last time, and the art director fussed with a spot on her glove.

"Everybody off the set!" Patrick commanded. "Now, Kelly. You look good on the Polaroid, but I need even more from you. This is not America, *chérie*. This if France, and you're a woman now. Come on, look at me like a woman. That's it! Hold it. Look off to the left. There's your lover coming to meet you! No, no—not some little boy from school. This is a man, a Frenchman. And France is a country of lovers, not schoolboys. Okay! Hold it! Fabulous. *Très bien!*"

Kelly did her best to show Patrick the expressions he wanted, but on the inside, she could hardly keep from laughing. A country of lovers? Is that what Patrick imagined himself to be, a lover? It wasn't Patrick she was thinking of, it was Eric. The fact that things were going better than ever between them. *Jen was right*, she thought. *Everything's different now that we're in Paris.*

When it was Nathalie's turn to go onto the set, Kelly watched as she was helped into her outfit: a long straight linen skirt, topped by an oversized blazer. The low, V neck and white fabric showed off her pretty olive-colored skin. Nathalie admired herself in the mirror, picking up Tristan's makeup brush to add some pink blush to her tanned cheeks.

"Careful, *chérie*." Tristan looked her over nervously. "You got enough color in Africa doing that movie last month. You'll come out too dark in the photographs."

"I am supposed to be dark, darling. Haven't you guessed Patrick's little scheme for Bonjour makeup? I am wearing winter white because I have the darkest coloring. Inge over there is summer. Bonnie is spring, with her strawberry-blond hair, and the little American"—she turned to appraise Kelly—"is autumn. Now aren't you surprised at how clever I am?"

Inge and Bonnie exchanged exasperated glances, but Kelly wished she'd guessed the scheme.

Just then, Patrick flipped the dressing room curtains aside and called out, "Where is my summer girl?" He looked right at Nathalie. "There is my beautifully tanned, sporty summer girl. That white linen suit is my favorite! Come on, darling, I told you there were plenty of gorgeous things for you to wear."

He took Nathalie by the hand and led her to the set. Passing Inge, he said to Tristan, "Go light on my ice-queen, yes?" Nathalie colored furiously, her explanation of the color scheme obviously dashed.

Bonnie burst into giggles. "That should teach her, that know-it-all!" Bonnie chuckled.

"I wish someone would tell off our little starlet," Inge agreed. "I can't imagine four long nights in the same studio with her!"

"Do you know her well?" Kelly asked.

"Only by reputation," Inge answered. "She was France's hottest model for about thirty-five minutes. Then she started her so-called film career, and she was the hottest new actress, for another brief moment!"

"Now, now girls," Tristan intervened. "She could be a very good actress. You have to admit that." He told Inge to close her eyes so he could finish her eye shadow. Kelly thought Inge really did look like an ice-queen, with her pearly-white skin and hair. And so far, she hadn't smiled much, either.

Nathalie came back from her shot and Bonnie went on the set. After that, Inge went on, dressed all in black, in striking contrast to her pale coloring. Soon, Kelly was on again, and then there were shots with two and three of them together. Inge and Bonnie continued to complain about Nathalie, but Kelly, fading fast, was too tired to make any more comments. By midnight, she thought she would drop from sheer exhaustion. She was just putting on her street clothes when Bonnie and Inge waved good-bye and left the dressing room together. Patrick was finishing his last shot of Nathalie. The day's shoot was finally over.

Kelly was too sleepy to try to avoid Nathalie when the French girl followed her out the studio door. "My, you take a long time to dress," Nathalie said, pulling a fox jacket around her shoulders. "Do all Americans take so long?"

"I wish you'd stop comparing me to 'all Americans.' I don't compare you to all the French," Kelly complained. She was too tired to be polite.

"I am not like all the French," Nathalie said airily. "I am not like anyone you have ever known."

"Didn't anyone ever tell you it's a real pain to listen to someone brag about themselves? No wonder you don't have any friends."

Nathalie stopped short. "Who told you I have no friends?"

"Nobody told me. I guessed." She glanced at Nathalie's face, then looked again. Unless she was mistaken, Nathalie seemed genuinely upset. "Listen," Kelly said uneasily, "it isn't any of my business. I'm sure you have plenty of friends."

"Of course I do," Nathalie said immediately. "Maybe not as many as you Americans . . . but . . ."

Kelly stared at her thoughtfully. "You might have more," she said carefully, "if you let someone else get a word in once in a while. No offense, Nathalie, but you talk too much. You act like no one else's opinion matters."

Nathalie shrugged. "Most people's opinions bore me."

Downstairs, at the entrance to the building, Kelly watched as Nathalie headed for a limousine waiting at the curb. Kelly scanned the street—there wasn't a taxi in sight.

"Oh, come on, you can ride with me," Nathalie said suddenly.

Feeling slightly guilty but also grateful, Kelly let Nathalie lead her to the limousine. She vaguely noticed the black-capped driver, the leather seats, and the passing lights of Paris. She was exhausted. The next thing she knew, they were at her hotel. She could hardly muster up the strength to move. Nathalie hadn't said a word to her the entire way home. Now she simply said, "*Bonsoir,*" as the driver helped Kelly out of the car.

When Kelly reached her room, she noticed the red light on her phone flashing. She called the message desk and was given a message from Eric: "Call me when you get up and we can have lunch and see a museum or something."

That would be nice, Kelly thought, *if I'm still alive tomorrow.*

She climbed out of her clothes, jumped into bed, and fell into a deep sleep. She never even bothered to wash the makeup off her face.

Four

The next morning Kelly was awakened by a loud knocking. At first, the noise seemed to be a part of her dream. Then suddenly she found herself awake in her huge, airy hotel bedroom, with a gold brocaded coverlet wrapped tightly around her. The knocking persisted, and Kelly heard her name called over and over.

"Just a minute!" she yelled, jumping out of bed and wrapping her terry cloth bathrobe around her.

When she opened the door, Simone stood there, her expression one of horror as she looked at Kelly's face. Kelly suddenly remembered that she was still wearing her makeup from the night before.

"*Bonjour*, Kelly. I tried to call late last night to see how the shoot went, but you did not answer."

Kelly rubbed the sleep out of her eyes and her mascara left globs of black all over her fingers. She felt disgusted and embarrassed. "I'm sorry, Simone. I got in so late last night, I've hardly had any sleep. I must not have heard the phone ring . . ."

"You must be a very sound sleeper," Simone said suspiciously. Kelly attempted a smile. "I understand you must be tired," Simone added. "But, my dear . . ." She glanced at Kelly's smudged eyes. "You must remember to wash your face at night. The Bonjour account is one of the biggest accounts in France. It calls for the clearest skin. You cannot possibly have that if you sleep with your makeup on!"

Kelly wrapped her robe tighter around her and wished the woman would go away. It was absurd to be roused out of needed sleep only to be criticized for her sleeping habits! Besides, Kelly felt horrible. She longed for a hot bath and wondered impatiently how long Simone was going to stay.

"I've never done this before," Kelly tried again. "You see, I . . . It was the longest day, and . . ." Suddenly she didn't know what to say.

Hunger overwhelmed her. "And I, uh . . . What time *is* it?"

"Twelve o'clock." Simone pursed her lips. "I will tell you what. You get dressed and meet me downstairs in the dining room. We can have a little talk and become better acquainted."

"Sure," Kelly agreed. "Great. See you downstairs."

She wanted to slam the door behind Simone. She'd never felt so intruded upon in her life! "Who does Simone think she is, anyway, to barge in on me like this?" she muttered aloud. Although, if it was already afternoon, Eric would be expecting her to call soon. She'd have to get going, anyway.

When she stepped into the luxurious bathroom and saw her reflection in the mirror, she let out a shriek. She looked like a raccoon. Her eyes were circled with black smudges and colors ran in streaks down her face. And her lips—she looked like a two-year-old who'd eaten a raspberry ice cream cone. No wonder Simone had looked horrified. *Thank goodness Simone wasn't Eric!* she thought. And she was supposed to be Meg Dorian's best! She had to giggle.

A half hour later, Kelly made her way to the hotel dining room, face scrubbed clean, hair neatly braided over one shoulder. Simone waved at her from the far end. Kelly couldn't wait for the agent to see her as she was now, a fresh-faced American girl.

She'd barely sat down at the table, however, when a waiter appeared carrying a cordless telephone. "Call for you, Mademoiselle." He placed the phone next to Kelly.

"I do not approve of phone calls during meetings," Simone said. But Kelly pointed out that it might be Meg Dorian, or even her own mother. She cradled the phone and turned as far away from Simone as she could, though it was impossible not to be overheard.

"Kelly—are you there?" a familiar voice asked.

"Eric!"

"Hi! You were supposed to call me when you woke up. Are we on for lunch?"

"I'm with my French agent," Kelly whispered. "I have to have breakfast with her."

"Okay—I get the hint. I'll come pick you up in, say, forty minutes."

"Make it an hour, okay? I'll see you."

"Who was that?" Simone seemed suspicious again as Kelly hung up the phone.

"It's the boy I know from home," Kelly said casually.

"That is exactly what I want to talk to you about." Simone looked at her sharply.

"You do?" Kelly felt uncomfortable. First Simone barged into her bedroom, and now she wanted to discuss her love life?

"Yes." Simone frowned severely, ignoring the waiter who poured her coffee. "We have often had trouble with our girls regarding boys. I know it is a big temptation for a girl traveling alone, but you have to remember the primary reason you are here."

"Wait," Kelly protested. "This isn't like that at all! Meg told you, didn't she, about my neighbors from home . . ."

Simone shushed her. "I know, each case is special, an exception. I have heard it all before. But you are only sixteen, Kelly, and we have our rules. Your mother should have come along on this trip. But she did not, so I must keep an eye on you."

"Of course," Kelly murmured in reply. What was the point of telling this woman that Eric lived across the street from her, that the only reason she'd been allowed to come to Paris was because his family was here? Simone seemed to ignore everything Kelly told her. Or maybe she simply didn't care.

The waiter came by with menus. Simone told him something in French before turning to Kelly. "I have a lunch date elsewhere. I thought we would just have tea or coffee and get to know each other."

"Oh," Kelly sighed in relief. She couldn't wait to get the meeting over with so she could meet Eric.

"So," Simone asked, "how did the Bonjour shoot go last night? Patrick is the most marvelous, creative photographer, is he not? And I trust you have met Nathalie? She is my star. Just a slip of a girl when I found her, but now she is the toast of Paris."

Kelly kept her mouth shut and listened patiently. Simone wasn't trying to get to know her at all—she was simply raving about Nathalie. Finally, Simone stood up, ready to leave. "I hope our little talk makes everything clear," she told Kelly before saying good-bye. "We will have no more trouble, yes? *Au revoir.*"

"*Au revoir,*" Kelly replied. *And good riddance,* she thought.

"Brother!" Kelly complained when she met Eric later in the hotel lobby. "Some meeting that was! All she did was warn me not to go out with boys and tell me what a big star Nathalie is. That's one of the models."

"She doesn't sound anything like Meg," Eric said sympathetically. "Are you sure it's okay for you to be seeing me?"

"Of course it is!" Kelly said hotly. She was already counting the hours they'd have together. It was one-thirty now, and she had to be at the studio at six. That left less than five hours to spend with Eric.

"What about that lunch I promised you?" Eric tugged Kelly's blue beret over her forehead. "I'm starving."

"Me, too." Kelly adjusted her beret, smiling shyly. Eric grabbed her hand and they left the hotel.

"Let's just start walking," Eric said impulsively. "We can stop to eat anywhere we like, okay?"

"Sure." They hurried down a narrow cobblestone sidewalk. Every girl who passed them on the street turned to look at Eric. Kelly was proud of him. *There's something about him*, she thought, *that even strangers notice*. From the corner of her eye, she peered at his tall, athletic build. He'd always been handsome, but there was a new self-assurance about him. Was it just because he was in Paris?

Kelly brushed her hair back over one shoulder as another teenaged Parisian girl gave Eric an appreciative glance. She wasn't exactly sure what it was, but these girls had style. Kelly was determined to try some of their tricks as soon as she got back to her room. In the meantime, she pulled her beret low over one eye, fished a new, fun pin from her purse, and attached it to the front of her beret. *It isn't so much what the Parisian girls wear*, she decided, *it's the way they wear it*.

"I thought we could explore Le Jardin des

Tuileries first, since it's so near your hotel," Eric suggested.

Kelly nodded enthusiastically, and they made their way down to the beautiful Jardin des Tuileries. Although Kelly had read that this was one of the smaller formal gardens in Paris, she thought it was absolutely charming and elegant.

Eric suggested lunch afterward. Kelly was hungry, but she didn't want to waste any sight-seeing time sitting down.

They ended up buying fresh crêpes from a street vendor. It seemed like a good idea at first, but as the thick jelly filling oozed out on her fingers, Kelly wished they'd gone to a regular restaurant instead.

"They're pretty messy," Eric said, coloring as he tried to lick the dripping jelly off his hands.

"Aren't they?" Kelly turned aside to dab at her mouth with a crumpled napkin. She caught Eric's eye and dissolved into helpless giggles.

As they were finishing eating, they overheard a group of British tourists discussing their visit to a nearby church. ". . . and its stained-glass windows were quite breath-taking," a balding man with two cameras slung around his neck was saying.

"This sounds interesting," Eric whispered to Kelly. He shyly sidled up to the photographer. "Excuse me, sir," he said politely, "but I couldn't help overhearing you discussing that church. Could you tell me how to get to it?"

"Certainly!" the man boomed heartily. "It's called La Sainte Chapelle, and it's possibly the most beautiful church in all of Paris. It's on L'Ile de la Cité, which is a small island between the Left and Right banks of the Seine."

"I've heard of it," Eric said. "Is it far from here?"

"Not at all. Just walk down along the Seine a little further until you come to the Pont Neuf. If you cross over that bridge, you'll be on Ile de la Cité. Once you're there, you can't miss the church."

Eric thanked the man, then hurried to join Kelly. "It sounds easy to get to. Want to take a look?"

"Sure," Kelly agreed. She took his hand and they waved goodbye to the group of tourists. They then made their way briskly along the Seine.

"Some people are so friendly, aren't they?" Eric commented. "That English guy sure was helpful."

"How could someone *not* be nice to you, Eric?" Kelly teased.

They soon spotted the Pont Neuf and eagerly crossed over to the Ile de la Cité. Just as their guide had predicted, they had no trouble finding La Sainte Chapelle.

Kelly squeezed Eric's hand in anticipation as they joined the crowds entering the thirteenth-century church. Inside, they stood stock still. The chapel was the most beautiful place Kelly had ever seen in her life.

Unconsciously, Kelly stood a little closer to Eric. He seemed oblivious of her. His face was rapt as he concentrated on the magnificent stained-glass windows that surrounded them. The panels were filled with scenes of life in biblical times. The sun streamed through the windows, highlighting the intense colors.

"It's like being inside a kaleidoscope," Kelly said softly. She turned to Eric. She was near enough to see the softness in his eyes. Then he pulled her close and kissed her.

A sudden clatter and the sound of voices shattered the moment. A tour group was all around them. Kelly and Eric burst into laughter. With Kelly in tow, Eric rushed headlong out of the chapel.

They came to a halt outside the church, flushed and out of breath. Eric squeezed Kelly's hand and kissed her cheek. "Let's just stay here forever," he told her. "We could spend all our days right on this island."

"We couldn't afford my hotel," Kelly pointed out. "This street could get awfully cold at night."

"We won't stay in the street," Eric scoffed. "We'll stay in Sainte-Chapelle."

"Why, Eric!" Kelly looked up at him, surprised at his romanticism. He'd never said anything like that at home. Unsure of what to say, she fumbled for a joke. "But the tourists would wake us up every morning."

Eric broke into a laugh. "I guess they would. Want to get some café au lait?"

"I'd love some." *Now, why did I do that?* she thought. *He was just about to say something important, I know it.* This was a side of Eric she'd never seen before—and she liked it.

Eric took her arm and guided her to a café across the street. Inside was the noise of laughing people, the ring of pinball machines, and a heavy smell of tobacco smoke. Eric led her to a small table near the window where they could look at the people passing on the sidewalk in front of them.

"I could easily spend the rest of my life in the cafés here just watching people walk by," he told her.

"People-watching!" Kelly laughed. "Isn't it a little rude to stare at people constantly?"

"The French are pretty good at it," Eric explained. "They love to sit at these cafés, especially in the summertime, and study everyone who passes by."

"Well—I would hate that!"

"You're a model—you're supposed to be used to

having people stare at you." Eric laughed. "Aunt Cecile says people here get all dressed up just to walk past the cafés."

The waiter came, and while Eric ordered café au lait for the two of them, Kelly marveled at all the new things around her. Including Eric. He seemed totally at ease in this foreign city. At home, Kelly often felt much more sophisticated than Eric. But here, Eric seemed both relaxed and excited, as if a new world had opened up to him.

The waiter placed two steaming bowls of milky coffee in front of them. Eric paid and Kelly waited until the waiter had gone. "Coffee in bowls?" she asked.

"Because of the milk," Eric explained. "The French drink it like this for breakfast."

"Eric—you're better than having a tour guide!"

Eric grinned. "You know—I never had a chance to find this out before, but I love to travel! Maybe when I'm through with college, I'll look for a job that will let me travel often."

"Models travel a lot, too," Kelly said without thinking. Then she blushed. She'd sounded as if she were inviting herself along on his future job! "I mean, I enjoy traveling, too. Except that I don't handle it as well as you do. I seem to get myself into the most awful situations. They're always funny afterward, but . . ." She shook her head, grinning.

Eric's hand closed over hers. "I'll protect you," he said gallantly.

Kelly felt a warm, happy glow that stayed with her all through the afternoon.

Five

That evening, preparations began again for a
night shoot at the Villanova Studio. Messengers
came and went, dropping off their precious cargo
of designer fashions.

"We'd better say good-bye out here," Kelly
murmured, pulling Eric to one side as a messen-
ger passed them in the narrow hallway.

"I wish I could come in. I've never seen you at
work."

"Not this time," Kelly told him. "You shouldn't
even be here now. If Simone dropped by, I'd be
dead."

"She won't drop by." Eric tugged Kelly's blue

beret, then kissed her. "That's for good luck," he said. He kissed her again.

"What was that for?"

"Uh, that was just for fun. But this"—he leaned closer—"this is for being the prettiest girl in Paris."

"Ahem." Someone cleared her throat loudly, and Kelly pulled away, certain it was Simone. Instead she found Nathalie staring at her—or rather, at Eric—with unabashed curiosity.

Eric flushed red, as shy as ever. Kelly felt a burst of anger. Nathalie had managed to ruin their good-bye, and for all she knew, Nathalie would tell Simone about finding her with Eric.

"I'd better run," Kelly told him. "I'll call you later."

As Eric left, Kelly grabbed Nathalie's arm. "Promise me you won't say a word about this to anyone."

"About this?" Nathalie looked at Kelly innocently and shrugged. "What is one little kiss? I promise—I will not say anything about this kiss."

Kelly breathed a sigh of relief. "Good. Then let's get to work."

As they walked into the dressing room, Tristan was already at work on Bonnie's makeup. Bonnie mumbled, "Hello," around the brush on her lips. Inge sat on a stool facing the long dressing-room mirrors, her face in her hands and a sulk on her pretty mouth. Kelly thought Patrick had been right to call Inge the ice-queen. The way she looked tonight, she could freeze anyone's heart.

Tristan finished Bonnie's makeup, and she got up off her stool.

"What's with Inge?" Kelly whispered.

"Oh, boyfriend trouble, what else?" Bonnie declared.

"Who's her boyfriend?" Kelly asked.

"Who knows?" Bonnie said. "Inge is very closemouthed about some things."

Kelly glanced at Inge again. She could imagine the kind of boyfriend Inge would have. He would be tall and blond, with a slim build, just like Inge herself.

Nathalie, removing the furs that covered her from head to toe, laughed at them all. "Inge has no real boyfriend," she said gaily. "Poor baby— nobody loves her."

"Nathalie!" Bonnie shrieked. Inge gave Nathalie a poisonous look, then continued to stare at the mirror and sulk.

"*Chérie*, your makeup, please." Tristan pulled at Kelly's elbow, motioning for her to sit down. "We don't want Monsieur Villanova mad at us." Kelly thought she saw Inge start at the mention of Patrick's name, but Nathalie chose that moment to grill her about the night before.

"Did you sleep well, or did you go out all night?" she wanted to know.

"Out all night?" Kelly gasped. "I was dead tired. I went right to sleep!"

"Oh . . . does not your boyfriend take you out at night?" Nathalie said innocently. All heads, including Inge's turned to Kelly. She was furious.

"Yes, but he also takes me out during the day," Kelly said coldly. "We have fun together. We don't have to do anything fancy. At least I know he cares about me!"

Nathalie colored deeply. "Many men care for me," she shot back. "And I can have any man I want, too!"

Bonnie laughed outright. "Then where's your engagement ring, love?" Bonnie held up her left hand, showing off the sparkling ring Kelly had noticed before.

"Is that an engagement ring?" Kelly asked. "It's beautiful."

Even Inge got up to admire Bonnie's ring.

"How lovely," she said enviously. "Diamonds and opals—it seems very special."

"It is," Bonnie agreed. "It belonged to Derek's grandmother. It's one of a kind. I just love it."

"You're lucky to have someone who loves you so much," Inge told Bonnie sincerely. "Derek must be wonderful."

"What a fuss over nothing," Nathalie said scornfully. "If it was his grandmother's, he did not even have to buy it."

"You're horrible!" Bonnie gasped.

"You don't know when to stop, do you?" Kelly faced Nathalie in disgust.

"Kelly, please . . . ," Tristan pleaded, turning her head back toward him.

"She's just jealous," Bonnie said haughtily.

"What's all the noise about?" Patrick rushed into the dressing room. "Tristan, are you taking your sweet time again? I need the girls on the set right away. Bonnie, is your makeup done? Then get dressed! Nathalie, Inge, Kelly, you hurry!"

"I'm working as fast as I can," Tristan protested. "You don't want a rush job, do you? For quality work, I need more time."

"I want quality work in a hurry," Patrick insisted sternly. "Bonnie, start dressing now. Kelly and Inge—I want you there in five minutes. Nathalie—ten minutes."

"*O, là là!*" Tristan hurried with Kelly's blush-on, almost dropping the little pot he was using. "They never give me the time to do things right." His fussing didn't prevent Kelly from seeing Patrick tweak Inge's cheek. "Cheer up, ice-princess," he told her.

"Ignore her, *chéri!*" Nathalie grabbed onto Patrick's arm. "She is just sulking to get your attention. She is so childish."

Patrick put his hand over Nathalie's. "Don't you worry about Inge. Just tell me why you were so late tonight."

"Kelly was just as late," Nathalie pouted. "Besides, Tristan is still busy with the makeup for the little American. Why should I have been any earlier, anyway?"

Patrick sighed. "Well, get busy now—start your own makeup. We have a lot of shooting to do tonight."

"Of couse, *chéri*." Nathalie smiled prettily at him and shook her head. "See my new earrings? They are going to dazzle our clients!"

"You know better than that. The stylist has already chosen your jewelry for the shots. You should leave all your personal jewelry at home."

"What a waste," Nathalie complained bitterly, removing the glittering rhinestone clips from her ears.

Something about the way Nathalie complained caught Kelly's attention. It was as if Nathalie felt personally rejected, just because Patrick didn't care about her earrings. That wasn't the way a self-confident film star would have acted. But a sudden shriek from Bonnie made her forget Nathalie.

"My hair is caught in this zipper!" the English beauty wailed as she struggled with her dress. "Help, someone!"

Inge and Kelly moved first. Bonnie's strawberry-blond hair was badly snarled in the zipper. They did what they could to disentangle her, but five minutes later, a lot of hair was still stuck.

Patrick, practically screaming, yelled from the studio. "Bonnie! Girls! Hurry up!"

"Goodness, he's going crazy!" Bonnie wriggled frantically. Kelly pulled a few more strands of hair out of the zipper, but the rest was still a matted mess, and getting worse all the time as she and Inge struggled with it.

"Bonnie! *Now!*" Patrick yelled.

"Photographers can be so unreasonable," Kelly complained to Inge.

She expected Inge to agree with her, but she was wrong. Inge just gave her a strange look and went back to the zipper.

"Oh, what am I going to do?" Bonnie moaned. "And I've got a shampoo commercial in London next week."

Nathalie, who'd been sitting quietly while Tristan worked on her makeup, came over. "I know what to do. Hold still." She pointed a pair of Tristan's cutting shears at Bonnie's smooth head.

When Bonnie saw the shears, she shrieked wildly. "Don't you come near me with those! So help me, if you don't put those things down, I'll cut your nose off!"

Nathalie looked as though she'd been slapped in the face. "I was just trying to help . . ." She faltered. "I know how to cut hair out of zippers so that you cannot even tell it has been cut."

"Oh, sure." Bonnie glared at her. "Tell me another one." Inge was watching Nathalie suspiciously, too. But something in Nathalie's expression gave Kelly the feeling that Nathalie really had meant to help. Still, Kelly couldn't blame Bonnie for not trusting her, not after the cruel things she'd said only minutes before.

"Never mind, Nathalie," Kelly said impulsively. "We'll manage." Instead of looking grateful, Nathalie glared at Kelly.

"Here, *chérie*, let me." Tristan took the shears from Nathalie. After some considerable trimming, the ill-fated hair was released from the zipper. Bonnie wailed when she saw the pieces of hair on the floor. "It took years for it to grow out of a layered cut! And my commercial!"

"It's in the back, you can hardly see it," Kelly consoled her. "It had to be done, honest. The hair was hopelessly stuck, wasn't it, Inge?" She turned to Inge, who nodded in agreement. Now that the excitement was over, Inge seemed as depressed as ever. Nathalie was also quiet, sitting by herself and pouting.

"So—is this little tea party at an end?" Patrick swung the dressing room curtains aside. "All of you—out on that set right now! Bonnie, it's no wonder the English economy does so badly with the way you British waste time!" Next he turned on Kelly. "And why are you not dressed? I had you flown all the way to Paris because of your reputation for being a hard worker. Well, I was wrong." Now he swung around to face Inge. "And if you do not melt that icicle hanging off your nose, I shall personally break if off!" He stomped back through the curtains. "If you are not on that set in thirty seconds flat, you are all fired!"

Kelly sat stunned at his tirade. Inge burst into sobs, while Bonnie, flushed, hurriedly tore the engagement ring off her finger and stuffed it into her bag. "I'm ready," she shouted at Patrick, disappearing into the studio.

"I'll be out in a second," Kelly said. Before changing out of her own clothes, she glanced again at Nathalie. Suddenly, Kelly saw her not as the horribly jealous and spiteful girl she'd been acting, but as a very sad and lonely young woman.

But Nathalie, catching Kelly's eye, snapped at her. "You are supposed to be getting dressed," she said, so nastily that Kelly forgot the pity she'd felt toward her just a minute before.

Bonnie did her solo shot while Kelly hustled into her dress. In a minute, Kelly was posing on the set, and then Inge went on, dressed in a dark gown that suited her sullen mood. Kelly grimaced. Patrick began shouting directions at Inge, to "Smile, smile." Anybody could see that Inge was in no mood for smiles. Her gown had a sophisticated, somber look that called for a soft, romantic mood. Why did Patrick insist that Inge smile?

Kelly and Bonnie lingered by the coffee machine to watch Inge being photographed. They must have had the same thought—that the Swedish girl might need support. Patrick was really giving her a hard time.

"Are you stupid?" he berated her loudly. "I told you to lift your head, not your hand!" Patrick glared from behind the camera, clicking nonstop and yelling at Inge. "Smile!" he insisted. "Is this a funeral?"

Inge, even paler than usual, tried to obey, but her expression was pitiful. She raised her hand to her face again, and again Patrick yelled at her to drop it. "No," she screamed back, holding her face in both hands. Suddenly Kelly saw the reason Inge had kept lifting her hand—to wipe her tears away!

"That creep!" Bonnie fumed. "He must know Inge is having boyfriend trouble, and he's purposely giving her a hard time! I can't believe he's this mean!"

"Between him and Nathalie, this shoot is a disaster," Kelly muttered.

Bonnie looked at her. "I should have known it would be like this. Derek wanted me to take a London job instead, but I thought a week in Paris would be fun. It really isn't worth it."

"Handkerchief!" Patrick called out. "Will someone please get a handkerchief!"

"I will," Kelly offered. She ran toward the

dressing room, bewildered at the way Patrick had purposely upset Inge.

Kelly opened the dressing room curtains, and found herself staring at Nathalie, fully dressed, bent over the tote bags that they all had stashed in a corner of the crowded room. She seemed startled when she saw Kelly come in but immediately regained her composure.

"I was just looking for some gum." She smiled brightly. "You would not have any, would you?"

"Gum? No," Kelly said, still distracted. "I need some tissues—for Inge."

"Here." Nathalie reached for a tissue box and handed it to Kelly. "What happened? Did her makeup run?"

"I don't know," Kelly mumbled, grabbing the tissue box. Nathalie picked up her own bag and tucked something inside.

"Where's Tristan?" Kelly asked suddenly.

"How should I know?" Nathalie patted her hair, gazing into the mirror. "I cannot keep track of everyone. Is Patrick ready for my shots yet?"

"I don't know," Kelly answered smoothly, "I can't keep track of everyone, either."

Nathalie snorted and gave Kelly a look of complete surprise. *People don't usually talk back to her*, Kelly realized. Then Nathalie yawned loudly. "Well, let us get to work. It is less boring than waiting around."

For the rest of the evening, they all worked

hard. Inge's crying spell was forgotten, and Patrick's mood had improved by the time they were through for the night.

Kelly had the last few setups to herself. By the time she got back to the dressing room, Tristan, Inge, and Nathalie were nowhere to be seen. Bonnie was on the floor, searching madly through her bag, a look of near-hysteria on her face.

"Bonnie, what's the matter?" Kelly knelt next to her. "Did you lose something?"

"No, I'm sure it's here. It's got to be here . . . Oh, no. It's just not possible . . ."

"What happened?" Kelly placed a hand on Bonnie's arm. "Tell me."

"My ring," Bonnie wailed. "I can't find my ring! Oh, Kelly, if I've lost it, I just don't know what I'll do. I thought I put it in here, but I was so frazzled before. It's Patrick's fault, yelling at me that way!"

"Are you sure it isn't there? I remember seeing you take it off. It must be around here somewhere."

"But it isn't! It just isn't here!" Bonnie's wails were more desperate. "How can I tell Derek? That ring was precious to him—he'll never trust me again!"

"Don't tell him yet," Kelly advised. "We'll find it, I'm positive."

They looked again through Bonnie's bag. They looked in her coat. They looked on Tristan's makeup counter. They searched the floors. But they didn't find the ring. Bonnie was in tears, and finally, Kelly suggested she go home and get some sleep. There was no point in looking any longer.

"You'll be fresh and calm tomorrow," Kelly told her. "You could come early and search the whole studio."

"You're right," Bonnie said gratefully. "I'm sure I'll find the ring then. Thanks so much, Kelly."

"You're welcome," Kelly said distantly. She didn't want to tell Bonnie what she really thought, just in case she was wrong. But as Bonnie left the dressing room, Kelly had a terrible feeling that Bonnie wouldn't find her ring at all, and for a very simple reason. The beautiful engagement ring, Kelly feared, wasn't in the studio anymore—it was in Nathalie's bag.

Kelly couldn't dismiss the image of Nathalie going through Bonnie's bag. She tried to push the thought from her mind. Why would Nathalie, who owned fur coats and a seemingly endless supply of jewelry, be tempted to take Bonnie's ring? It made no sense . . . except . . . Bonnie had teased Nathalie, had flaunted her engagement in front of her. But that didn't justify stealing Bonnie's ring—not even as a joke. And Nathalie, Kelly knew, didn't have much of a sense of humor.

Six

Kelly arrived back at her hotel emotionally and physically exhausted. Patrick had worked her hard, doing nearly twenty shots that evening, and nit-picking about everything from her hair to her facial expressions. Kelly sighed as she stepped out of the taxi and headed for the lighted entrance of the luxurious hotel. The last thing she wanted was to get involved in accusing Nathalie of theft, and yet she didn't see any way out of it. Poor Bonnie was sick over losing the ring, and Kelly couldn't stand to hear her blame herself.

There was no use denying it; she had to help Bonnie. On the other hand, there was no actual proof that Nathalie had taken the ring. Kelly had seen enough mystery shows on TV to know things weren't always as they seemed. It was all so complicated, and she was just too tired to think about it anymore.

Kelly smiled at the night clerk. "Room sixty-one," she told him, holding her hand out for her room key.

"*Ah, bonsoir*, Mademoiselle. Room sixty-one." The clerk, a young man with a dark suit and blond hair neatly combed back, looked in the cubicle where her room key hung. "I believe you have a letter, Mademoiselle." He took out an envelope and handed it to Kelly. "*Voilà!*"

Kelly ripped open the envelope and smiled as she recognized the familiar scrawl.

"Your secret admirer awaits! Call him at midnight for a super spectacular, amazingly wonderful treat—XXX OOO."

Laughing outright, Kelly hurried to her room, where she kicked off her shoes and dialed Eric's uncle's phone number. Eric answered right away.

"Hi!" His voice was wonderful to hear. She felt less troubled already. "Did you get my note?"

"I'm not sure," Kelly teased. "I got a note from my secret admirer."

"I admire you," Eric quipped, "and that's no secret."

She felt a rush of warmth, and thought, *This is it—this is what being in love feels like. This is what I've dreamed about and waited for, all this time.*

It was peculiar, really. All the time she'd known Eric, all those months when she'd had such a terrible crush on him, she'd imagined she was already in love. But this was different. She knew that Eric felt the same way about her.

"So what's this wonderful treat," she asked lightly. "I'm supposed to be in bed. I have a curfew, you know."

"I know. But listen, Kelly, it's really only early evening—for us, that is. So I made plans to take you out tonight."

"Tonight? Now?"

"You sound so surprised! I thought you'd love the idea."

"Well, I guess I'm not as tired as I thought I was," Kelly admitted. "And you're right, it is only six o'clock back home. But I really shouldn't."

"Why not?" Eric wanted to know. "Does the front desk keep tabs on you?"

"Oh, no." Kelly laughed. "They don't care! But I promised Meg I'd behave. And Simone might barge in on me again tomorrow morning. She has this thing about clear skin and getting enough beauty sleep. As if I would wake up with wrinkles if I went to bed too late!"

Eric pressed his point. "The thing is, there's this little place where they play rock music. It's great, Kelly. You'd love it! Besides, you can sleep late tomorrow morning, or even take a nap after we go out for lunch. You don't start work till six P.M."

"Well . . ." Kelly hesitated. "I did promise . . ."

"You promised to get back to your hotel right after work," Eric said slyly, "but you didn't say anything about what you'd do afterward."

Kelly faltered. She'd promised Meg to keep early hours, but then again, it *was* early by New Jersey time. She could still get in seven or eight hours sleep, since she didn't have to get up until noon for her lunch date with Eric.

"I wouldn't put the pressure on," Eric continued, "except, well, this is *Paris*, Kelly. Just think, a night out, all alone, just the two of us, in Paris—when will that ever happen again?" He paused. "Besides, I"—his voice caught—"I really want to see you." Kelly made her decision.

Twenty minutes later, she'd scrubbed off her makeup, and changed into her jeans, a red cashmere sweater and a denim jacket. Eric was already waiting in the lobby when she stepped off the elevator. She couldn't get over how terrific he looked. He had on a new shirt, a gray-and-black tie, and his old black sport coat. He looked very European and sophisticated.

"Are you sure I'm not dressed too casually?" she asked.

"No, you're perfect." Eric smiled. "I was wondering when I was going to see the real Kelly Blake again!"

She wrinkled her nose at him. "So where are we going?" Kelly impulsively took his hand as they made their way to the desk clerk to drop off her key. The clerk looked at the two of them curiously. *It's one o'clock in the morning to him*, Kelly realized. *He's not operating on New York time.* Being with Eric had made her forget about the late hour.

"My uncle told me about this place," Eric explained. "It's in a basement, so they call it a *cave*. Tonight the group is playing some old rock, American-style, and some new songs they wrote themselves."

"Sounds terrific," Kelly agreed. She expected Eric to ask the doorman to hail a taxi, but a quick look told her the streets were empty.

"There are no cabs," she said, worried.

Eric laughed. "We don't need a cab tonight. I told you to expect a special treat." He led the way to a small side street around the corner. There, chained to a streetlamp, stood a shiny red moped. Eric took a key from his pocket and began to undo the lock.

"A moped!" Kelly squealed. "Where did you get it? Do you know how to drive it?"

"It's rented, and yes, I've had it all evening and I'm an expert driver by now. I wish I could afford a Porsche, or a limo, but this little machine has an excitement all its own."

"Oh, Eric!" Kelly threw her arms around his neck. "I couldn't think of a better way to see Paris." Eric drew her face close to his and gave her a long, lingering kiss under the light of the streetlamp. It was all she could do to break away. She almost didn't care about the nightclub.

"We'd better go now, or we'll never go," Eric said, echoing her own thoughts. He settled Kelly behind him and took off. As the moped swung onto the Champs-Elysées, Kelly looked over her shoulder at the Arc de Triomphe in the distance. Soon they passed the Place de la Concorde, a huge open square, where even at this hour cars seemed to follow no set path.

"I'm taking the long way around," Eric shouted, "so you can at least get to see some of Paris."

Kelly tightened her grip on his waist to let him know she'd heard.

Kelly was thankful that the streets were much emptier than during the day, as Eric maneuvered the tiny motorbike through narrow roads. Once again they crossed the Seine over the Pont Neuf. The wide river that divided Paris into two parts sparkled in the moonlight. On the Left Bank of Paris, the streets grew even narrower. As they threaded their way past cafés and tiny hotels, Eric honked the horn to warn pedestrians that the motorbike was coming through. They raced down the Boulevard Saint-Germain, which was as crowded with late-night strollers as if it were one-thirty in the afternoon, not one-thirty in the morning.

Kelly realized that Paris, like New York, was a city that never slept. At any hour of the day or night, something was going on somewhere. *And,* she thought with a smile, *we traveled thousands of miles to get here, just to find out what we'd guessed at home.*

"We're almost there," Eric shouted at the next traffic light. He turned the moped onto the Boulevard Saint-Michel. The Musée Cluny stood at the corner, spotlights illuminating the ancient ruins surrounding it. "This museum is dedicated to the art of the Middle Ages—I read it's probably the best collection of its kind." Eric's voice carried on the wind. "And the ruins of the baths date from Roman times!"

"Roman times!" Kelly looked in amazement. In New York there were historic buildings standing among the new, but at most, they were one or two hundred years old.

Eric turned off the wide boulevard and the narrow streets returned. Stopping in front of a nondescript door, he announced, "Here we are," and shut off the moped. "This is La Boîte de Cave. I think it means 'cave box.' Some name for a club, huh?" Kelly agreed the name was a bit strange.

They knocked on the unmarked door and a sinister-looking man let them in. The man's hair was cut in a Mohawk style, and a long cigarette dangled from his mouth. Eric slipped him a bill, and Kelly, who couldn't see what it was, wondered if she should pay her share. But Eric guided her firmly through the door, down some steps, and along a darkened corridor. Ahead, she could hear the loud booming of music.

As they approached the club, tobacco smoke drifted toward them. "I've noticed that the French smoke much more than Americans do," Kelly observed. Eric led her into the club, which really did look like a cave. The walls seemed to be made of solid stone, and there wasn't a window in sight. It was hard to make out the faces of the patrons because of both the smoke and the darkness, but it was obvious that the place was packed. People sat at tables and stood at the back, cheering the rock group that was performing at the far end of the room. A waitress appeared and led Kelly and Eric to a table. The noise was almost deafening at first, but after a few minutes Kelly's ears grew accustomed to it.

"What would you like to drink?" Eric asked.

"Uh—maybe some coffee?" she said. If Eric wanted a real drink, she didn't want to seem like a baby. In France, even children drank wine.

"I'll order for both of us." Eric said something to the waitress that Kelly couldn't hear.

The waitress soon returned with two mugs filled with steaming liquid. "Hey!" Kelly leaned toward Eric. "How did you know I love hot apple cider?"

"I know more than that about you." Eric turned to her with a smile.

Kelly felt Eric's arm tightening around her, and he moved his chair closer to hers. She put her head on his shoulder and sat like that for a while, watching the performers. The group's name translated as "Moving Forces." Their original music was on the political side, Kelly decided, though they also did a lot of old rock numbers. Kelly's favorites, though, were the more romantic numbers.

Eric was wearing after-shave lotion, and it smelled incredibly good. She turned her head and the tip of her nose touched Eric's face. He bent down and brushed his lips against her forehead. Then he kissed her again, right there in the club, with dozens of people around them. But nobody paid the least bit of attention. The music and smoke enveloped them all like a thick, warm blanket.

It was strange to realize that no one there cared what she and Eric did. They were really on their own. Kelly felt a bit dazed.

The musicians finished their set to loud, enthusiastic applause. Kelly watched as they put their instruments down and disappeared into the crowd. *They didn't play for long*, she thought. *Or at least, it didn't seem like a long time!* She hadn't worn a watch, and she didn't want to know what time it was. Not on one of the most perfect evenings of her life.

Eric picked a rose out of the vase of flowers on the table and tucked it behind Kelly's ear. Laughing, she took a second flower and tried to do the same to him. He twisted his head out of reach easily.

"Hey! Isn't that your friend?"

Startled, Kelly drew back. "What? Who?"

"That other model—the one we saw outside the studio this afternoon."

"Nathalie, here? Where?"

"Over there, in that corner."

Kelly turned her head. Sure enough, there was Nathalie, sitting at a small table with two other people. Even in the dimly lit room, Kelly could see that Nathalie looked especially beautiful tonight.

"She really is pretty," Eric murmured.

"Isn't she?" Kelly said. She hadn't said much to Eric about the personality clashes on the shoot; she hadn't wanted to spoil their good times together by complaining.

"Look. I think she wants to come over here."

Kelly hesitated. It would seem rude to ignore

Nathalie, now that they'd seen her; and maybe she could find out more about Bonnie's ring.

"Do you know those people she's with?" Eric asked.

Kelly took a closer look. "Oh, no. I don't believe it! Patrick and Inge are with her—the photographer and another model from my shoot. I guess I should go over and say hello."

"You really don't like them, do you?" Eric gazed at her quizzically.

"It's not that. I just realized that Patrick is probably Inge's boyfriend. I feel stupid that I didn't guess it before. Inge's been upset over him—they've obviously been fighting."

"Then maybe we should just leave them alone."

"I know," Kelly agreed, "but I wonder, why is Nathalie with them?"

"Beats me."

Kelly frowned. "She probably invited herself," she finally said. "She doesn't seem to have any friends. She has a hard time getting along with everyone."

"Patrick doesn't seem to think so."

At the other table, Nathalie was leaning close to Patrick, laughing loudly at something he had said, while Inge looked as sulky as ever.

"That's just like Nathalie!" Kelly exclaimed. "I've tried to give her the benefit of the doubt, but I don't trust her for a minute. She does nothing but flirt with men and insult all the women . . . and maybe worse." Kelly told Eric about Bonnie's ring, and about her suspicions that Nathalie had taken it.

"A thief?" Eric seemed incredulous.

"I said I wasn't positive."

"Do you really want to talk to her now?"

Kelly was already pushing back her chair. She waved at Nathalie and saw the other girl's face light up. "Come on," she urged Eric. "Let's just say hello. Maybe I can find out something about that missing ring."

"You'd better not try," Eric advised. "You don't have any proof that she took it, and it would be pretty embarrassing to accuse her if it wasn't true."

"You're right. I guess I won't say a word about it."

Eric was suddenly thoughtful. "Maybe this isn't such a bad idea after all. In fact, I'd like to talk to Nathalie myself. Come on."

As they moved to Nathalie's table, Kelly was a bit puzzled that Eric suddenly seemed so eager to speak to Nathalie. She reached up and took the red rose from behind her ear. It seemed silly now.

"Look who's here—our own little American, Kelly Blake." Nathalie looked directly at Eric.

Inge said hello politely as Kelly introduced Eric, but Patrick was obviously not happy to see them. Kelly guessed he'd had enough intrusions on his night with Inge. As if to confirm her suspicions, he rose as soon as everyone had been introduced and took Inge's hand.

"Nathalie, *chérie*, it looks as if you will not be alone after all. Come, Inge. Let us leave."

"But . . . but it is so early," Nathalie protested sweetly. "And we were all having such a lovely time."

"I think it's a good time to leave," Inge said coldly. Anyone could see that she was eager to get away from Nathalie. Kelly could feel the tension between them. Inge and Patrick would no doubt have a big fight over Nathalie as soon as they were alone.

Nathalie pouted prettily, then reached for Eric's arm and gave him a glorious smile. "I suppose it is all right. Now that I have such a handsome young man to talk to, no?"

Kelly wanted to yank Nathalie's hand off Eric. *Hold on*, she chastised herself, *stay calm. Nathalie is too flirtatious, but I trust Eric. What's wrong with me, anyway?*

Patrick nodded curtly and pulled Inge into the crowd. Soon they were completely out of sight.

"Well, Patrick was not such good company, anyway," Nathalie confided to Eric. "And that Inge." She shuddered. "She makes one's blood run cold."

"Not everyone can be as warm as the French," Eric said, without taking his eyes from her face.

Nathalie giggled and squeezed Eric's arm. "My, he is even nicer than I imagined," she said to Kelly. "What flattery!"

"I never flatter anyone who doesn't deserve it," Eric replied.

Kelly's mouth dropped open. She knew she was staring blatantly, but she couldn't help herself. Eric never acted this way! Abruptly, she stood up. "Well, Nathalie, this has been nice, but we'd better get back to our own table." Eric looked at her blankly. "Uh, the waitress won't know where to put our bill," she added.

"She'll find us," he said, gazing at Nathalie. "The place isn't that large."

"Well, but . . . we left our jackets over there."

"Sit down. They will be perfectly safe," Nathalie assured her. "We do not have the terrible crime here that you Americans have. No one will touch your jackets." She turned an ingratiating smile on Eric. "Tell me about yourself," she said in a soft, cajoling voice. "I would like to know everything about you. American boys are so darling!"

Eric actually began telling Nathalie about how he came to be in Paris! For a minute, Kelly simply stood there, stunned. Couldn't he tell what a phony Nathalie was? She was so obvious—she couldn't get a boyfriend of her own, so she latched onto everyone else's boyfriends. That was terrible enough. But that Eric would fall for her tricks was more than Kelly could stand.

"Eric, I . . ." She put a hand to her forehead. "I have a terrible headache. It's been coming on all night. I think we'd better go."

Eric stood up, frowning in concern. "I'm sorry, Kelly. Is it bad?"

"Very bad," she said, glancing at Nathalie.

"Why do you not try some coffee," Nathalie suggested sweetly. "Some people say that caffeine eases headache pain."

"I've never heard that," Kelly said stiffly. "I'd rather go back to the hotel for some aspirin."

"Oh, I have aspirin in my purse," Nathalie cried, hoisting the huge tote bag that she'd had in the studio that day.

"I'll bet you do," Kelly muttered. "And I'd like to know what else you have in there."

"Well, maybe we *should* go." Eric sprang to his feet. "I'll just take Kelly back to the hotel. She probably needs some rest . . . You know, jet lag and all."

Nathalie set her purse on the floor. "That is too bad," she said, batting her eyes at Eric. "We were having such an interesting talk."

"Maybe some other time," Eric said.

"Well, why not come back here after you drop off Kelly?" Nathalie looked at Eric so innocently Kelly wanted to scream. "I will probably be right here, listening to this wonderful music."

Without a word, Kelly turned on her heel, marched back to the other table, snatched up her jacket, and headed for the door. A minute later, Eric appeared beside her.

"Oh, look who's here," she said, her voice poisonously sweet. "Our darling American boy."

Eric laughed. "Come on—I can't believe Nathalie actually bothered you."

"Oh, no?" Kelly said furiously. "What would you believe, that Nathalie is as sweet and innocent as she acts?"

"You're jealous!" Eric grinned, delighted and smug. "Now I *am* flattered."

Kelly gasped. "Maybe I've been kidding myself. I thought I knew you, knew what you were really like. Oh, forget it, just forget it!" She stomped off and Eric followed.

"Kelly, come on. You're really overreacting."

"Am I?"

"Look, I know she's a flirt, but how are you going to find out if she took the ring if you don't talk to her?"

"I don't want to talk to her."

"And by the way, you almost blew it, with that line about what's in her purse. My uncle Didier says journalists have to be discreet. Face it, you weren't very subtle."

"Me, not subtle?" She could barely speak, she was so angry. "I suppose I should've been grateful to her."

"She was trying to be nice about your headache," Eric said impatiently. "Give her some credit."

"Okay, fine. You can tell her how grateful I am when you come back here later, like she wants you to do."

Eric leaned over to unlock the chain securing the moped. Kelly turned away, tears stinging her eyes. *He didn't even deny it. He didn't even bother to say he wouldn't dream of going back to the cave, that he has no interest in Nathalie!*

The ride home was tensely silent. This time, Kelly was grateful for the noise of the moped, because she couldn't talk—not to Eric, anyway. She hated Paris. She was sorry she'd ever come. It was too much of a strain, everything was so foreign, the people were so different. You couldn't trust anyone. She just wanted her job to be over so she could go home, be herself, and surround herself with people who really cared about her.

At the hotel, she ignored Eric's offer of help as she climbed off the back of the moped. Snubbing him completely, she marched into the lobby, picked up her room key, and headed straight for the elevators without once looking back.

"Kelly!" Eric reached for her arm as the elevator doors opened. She yanked her arm out of reach, stepped into the elevator quickly, and stabbed at the buttons. Why were the doors so slow?

"Kelly, it's too late to argue tonight. Let's discuss it tomorrow."

"Oh, don't worry about me," she said sarcastically. "I'm just fine." Thankfully, the door finally slid shut.

"I'll pick you up for lunch at noon, here in the lobby . . ." Eric's voice faded as the elevator climbed.

"Don't bother," she said to the elevator walls, tears rolling down her cheek. "Don't worry about me—worry about your precious Nathalie!"

Seven

Early the next morning Kelly woke with a start. For the second morning in a row, someone was pounding on her door.

"Hello?" she responded in a sleepy voice. Who could it be? Eric, apologizing for the abrupt way he'd left her the night before? She hoped so, but wondered why he'd come over so early. She was so tired, she could hardly wrap her robe around her before going to the door.

"Who is it?" she called.

"Kelly? It's Simone. Are you awake?"

Awake? Kelly could barely talk, and her mouth tasted like glue. "Not really," she muttered, opening the door to let the agent in. Simone peered closely at Kelly's face and examined the room as she stepped inside.

"I tried to call you late last night, but you were not in again." Simone was angry.

"I was here," Kelly lied, shaking her head to clear it. Simone would never understand that there was nothing wrong with her seeing Eric.

"I suppose you were fast asleep again," Simone said coldly. Clearly, she was in no mood for excuses.

"I guess I was." Kelly tried to sound convincing, but the lie seemed to stick in her mouth.

"Good," Simone said. "Then you are well-rested."

"I guess so," Kelly yawned. Well-rested? What a laugh. She felt simply horrible. She could smell the stale cigarette smoke that clung to her hair.

"Very good," Simone continued, "because the Bonjour people have decided to start early today. It is New Year's Eve tomorrow night, and there are still many shots to do. How quickly can you get ready?"

"What time is it?" When Simone turned her back, Kelly rubbed her eyes. They felt irritated, probably from the cigarette smoke and from riding the moped in the wind without goggles.

"It is after eight o'clock. If you were asleep by one, that is more than seven hours of sleep. You should be fine," Simone said evenly.

"I'm sure I will be," Kelly agreed uncertainly. There was no way she could admit that she hadn't gotten in until three-thirty the night before. She'd had barely four hours sleep, and she felt it. And now she had to pretend she felt like a million dollars for an entire extra-long day.

"What is the matter, Kelly?" Simone asked suspiciously. "You do not sound so sure. You *were* asleep at one o'clock, were you not?"

"Of course," Kelly insisted. "I really was."

"Good," Simone said. "It is not just that you need the proper rest. It is also that you are underage, and technically, I am responsible for you. I do not understand why Meg insisted you were responsible enough to take care of yourself. Clearly, I have to keep tabs on you." Simone paused. "Then I can tell Patrick we will be at the studio at nine o'clock?"

"Nine o'clock?" Less than an hour to wash her hair, eat breakfast, and make it over to the studio! How could this happen, today of all days? And worst of all, she couldn't possibly call Eric to ask him about last night, not with Simone hanging over her. All her questions would have to wait until her lunch break—if she even got one!

"*Très bien.* Now, let us hurry." Simone clapped her hands together.

"Will we have any time off?" Kelly asked Simone.

"What do you mean—what time off?"

"Time off for lunch."

"Of course you will have time to eat lunch. We are not barbarians, we are just trying to get this job done."

"I appreciate that," Kelly said, heading for the bathroom. Good—she'd have a lunch break, she could meet Eric and . . .

What am I thinking? Memories of the night before flooded into her mind. *Eric won't want to have lunch with me, not after the way I acted last night. I was such a dope. I can't believe I thought he'd go back to see Nathalie. He never would. Would he?*

In the clear morning light, her jealousy the night before seemed ridiculous. Eric had never made her jealous before, and there were certainly plenty of pretty girls back home who would give him the chance. *But they aren't beautiful French models*, Kelly thought.

Stop it! She held on to the edge of the sink and closed her eyes. She was too sleepy to think straight, that's what it was. Her mind wavered—Eric was loyal, Eric was naive. Eric loved her, Eric had fallen for Nathalie's tricks. Kelly thrust her hands over her ears, as if that would stop the thoughts from careening wildly around in her head.

Simone pounded on the bathroom door. "What

are you doing in there? We do not have much time!"

Kelly turned on the faucets as hard as they could go. "Washing," she yelled. "Washing up."

Patrick's studio in less than an hour! Some advance notice she'd gotten. Of course, Simone did say she'd tried to get her last night. As tired as she was, Kelly had to admit that it was her own fault that she'd never gotten the call.

They didn't get to the studio until a quarter after nine, and Patrick immediately screamed at her. "You are late!" He was acting as cranky as she felt. In a corner of the dressing room, Inge sat, dark circles marring her pretty, pale features. Bonnie, obviously still upset over her lost ring, was pouting as Tristan applied her makeup. Nathalie was even later than Kelly, arriving at nine-thirty with her hair looking as if she hadn't bothered to comb it. Patrick, however, didn't say a cross word to her, only scowled slightly when she kissed him good morning.

Inge turned away as Nathalie entered the dressing room. Nathalie didn't let Inge snub her, however.

"Inge, *chérie*. We are up early this morning, are we not? I trust you got plenty of sleep last night?"

Inge cursed Nathalie under her breath. Bonnie, who obviously hadn't gotten much sleep herself, immediately began talking about her lost ring. She was furious because the stepped-up schedule hadn't given her a chance to search the studio privately.

"Please, it is too early for your whining," Nathalie snapped. She turned to Kelly with a smirk. "Some of us were up quite late last night."

Kelly felt a strong urge to tell Nathalie to shut her mouth. But she knew that if she did, Nathalie would go running to Simone and tell all. It wasn't worth another of Simone's lectures.

"How late?" Simone demanded as she walked into the dressing room.

"Oh, Simone," Nathalie said lightly. "I was just teasing. I am sure Kelly got just as much sleep as I did."

Kelly felt helpless. She had to find out if Eric had gone back to see Nathalie or not. She couldn't quite believe he had, but then again, Eric had changed so much since be came to Paris. No, he couldn't have changed that much. It was all Nathalie's fault—she had a way of making Kelly doubt herself.

Kelly would have loved to tell Simone the truth about where Nathalie had been the night before. Unfortunately, she couldn't do that without getting herself into trouble. Across the room, Nathalie winked at her. They were partners, the wink seemed to say, and Kelly felt both angry and confused. If only she'd talked to Eric last night, instead of sending him off in silence! She'd never felt more uncertain. Nathalie was a lot more clever than she'd thought.

Meanwhile, Inge had cornered Bonnie. "What's this about your ring?" she asked.

"My beautiful engagement ring. It was here yesterday. Remember, I took it off right before my setup? But later, I couldn't find it. Kelly and I looked everywhere for it. I thought, maybe, you saw it, or put it somewhere . . ."

"I'm sorry, I know nothing about it."

"What am I going to do?" Bonnie wailed.

Tristan pulled Bonnie's hand away from her face. "It's too bad you lost your ring, but don't ruin your makeup now, okay?" He motioned for Kelly to take the seat Bonnie had vacated. Kelly sat down gratefully, studying the colorful little pots of lipstick, blush, and eyeshadow Tristan had displayed on the counter. As Tristan started her foundation, applying a soft beige base to her face with light, even pats, Kelly looked at Inge, who was sitting at the counter pretending to read a magazine. Kelly had noticed how she'd flinched when Nathalie came in. If Patrick was the only man in Inge's life, she felt sorry for the girl; he seemed to make her so miserable. Kelly couldn't imagine what Inge saw in Patrick, anyway. These few days of working with him had proved he was an arrogant egotist. What kind of girl would be attracted to a man like that? But many photographers seemed to have their pick of women; Kelly had already noticed that in her brief experience as a model. Patrick didn't seem worth it! What right did he have to make Inge so unhappy?

Kelly looked at Inge's downturned mouth, her sad blue eyes lined with rings of gray. She was furious with Nathalie all over again. Nathalie had probably made things even worse for Inge by flirting with Patrick the night before. She seemed determined to ruin everyone's relationships.

It was nearly eleven o'clock by the time Kelly was ready to go onto the set. Tristan had done her makeup sixties-style; dark eyes with black eyeliner and heavy mascara, white skin, and pale, pearly-pink lips. He had straightened her hair so that it lay almost flat against the side of her face. The finished result was quirky and cute. She had the doll-like look of the London models of the sixties: long black stretch pants that fit like stockings, flat patent-leather shoes, even pink polka-dot stockings peeking through the stirrups of the pants. But the best and wildest part of the outfit was the jacket. It was hip length and made of a fuzzy material that reminded Kelly of pink cotton candy. An assistant lifted the jacket's pink hood over her hair, and Tristan rushed at her with a comb. Finally, he looked her over approvingly.

"You look just like one of those Beatle girls," he said.

"Beatle girls!" Kelly laughed. "My mom says she had a crush on Paul McCartney when she was a teenager. But I never thought of her as a Beatle girl!"

For the first time since she'd lost her ring, Bonnie laughed, her cheeks glowing pink. "In England, everybody's mum was a Beatle girl at one time or other. My own mother had a pink jacket just like that one. Funny, isn't it, how things come back in style!"

"I would never wear that kind of junk," Nathalie declared. "It looks cheap."

Bonnie put her hands on her hips and frowned. "Not everybody can afford to walk around in real fur, you know. Or perhaps your furs were a gift from an admirer?"

Kelly pulled Bonnie aside. "Stop it, both of you," she said.

"You're siding with her?" Bonnie gasped in disbelief.

"I'm not siding with anyone," Kelly insisted. "I just can't stand this kind of arguing. We have to finish this job together, no matter how we feel about each other. Maybe we should all keep our opinions to ourselves, for a while at least. Just forget about Nathalie, okay, Bonnie?"

"You're right," Bonnie said with a sigh. "I don't care for Nathalie, but it's not her fault about the ring."

"Right." Kelly smiled. "It'll be much nicer around here now—you'll see."

As Kelly was heading for the set, Nathalie bent down in front of her as if to pick up something she'd dropped. Straightening up, she whispered to Kelly, "Thank you." Then she took her place at the makeup counter.

Kelly stared after her—had she heard correctly? Had Nathalie actually thanked her? She felt a twinge of conscience: could it be she'd judged Nathalie too harshly?

The backdrop on the set featured the Bonjour makeup products in all their splendor: a giant poster showed blushers, eye shadows, eyeliners, and dozens of shades of lipsticks.

"At last," Patrick sighed as Kelly came into view. "I was getting rather tired of all those dresses. It is about time I had something interesting to shoot."

"Thanks for the compliment," Kelly drawled. She was in no mood for Patrick's jokes. Her heavy black makeup hid some of the dark circles under her eyes. But she still felt awful. Patrick looked even worse. He had bags under his eyes and his face was lined and yellow-looking. She wondered if he and Inge had patched things up between them.

Fabian took a light-reading, and Patrick set his camera. "Now, Kelly—you are in the magical land of makeup. You are Little Pink Riding Hood in Candy Land, and you are having the time of your life. Whee—here is a candy lipstick. You are going to hop, skip, and jump through Candy Land. There you go, Kelly! That's it! Lots of smiles, hops, leaps, jumps. Hold your hood. Smile! Right knee up. That's it!"

As much as Kelly disliked Patrick personally, she had to admit that he had talent. His cues helped her to forget how tired she was. But in the back of her mind, all morning long, was a niggling fear about Eric. *Is he trying to ruin everything we had going for us?* She wondered. *Or am I?*

Eight

Patrick kept Bonnie and Kelly after the other models had gone out to lunch in order to shoot a small insert. It was nearly twelve-thirty by the time they were given permission to break for lunch.

All Kelly could think about was Eric. Would he be waiting for her in the hotel lobby as he'd promised? By the time she got there she'd be forty-five minutes late. Would he think she'd stood him up? Kelly recalled the time they'd had a date to go to the movies, and she'd gotten stuck in the city without a chance to tell him the date was off. And then there was the time she'd turned him down for a ride home from a shoot because a movie star being photographed with her was interested in her. Kelly's conscience tweaked her. *Of course, that was before we were really going together,* she thought. *He must know I wouldn't stand him up now.* But she couldn't be sure. After last night, Eric might think she was breaking their date because she was still angry.

Patrick snapped his fingers under her nose. "What is your problem? Pay attention and we will finish sooner."

"I—I have an appointment at my hotel," Kelly stuttered, "and I'm terribly late. I'm afraid I'll miss . . . uh, them."

"So, when this shot is finished—which I hope will be immediately—call the hotel," Patrick growled. "We have telephones in France."

Kelly smacked her hand against her forehead. "What a dope I am! Of course!"

As soon as Patrick said, "That's it," Kelly ran to the telephone.

Hôtel Gabriel," a voice replied. *"Réception."*

"Yes, hello." She tried to sound calm. "This is Kelly Blake, of room sixty-one."

"Ah, yes, Mademoiselle Blake. What may we do for you?"

"I'm running late for an appointment. Is there a young man there, waiting for me? Or a message?"

"No message, Mademoiselle, but there was a young man asking for you earlier . . ."

"Is he still there?" Kelly replied excitedly. "I'd like to talk to him, please."

"Well, I am afraid that would not be possible." The desk clerk sounded both serious and slightly amused.

Kelly felt herself start to panic. "He didn't leave, did he?"

"Well, yes, I am afraid so."

"But"—Kelly moaned—"I'm only half an hour late. He could have waited! And he didn't leave a message?"

"No, Mademoiselle Blake. Would you like to leave a message in case Monsieur returns?"

"No, thank you." She quickly made up her mind: she'd go over to the hotel right now in case Eric did return.

Back in the dressing room, Bonnie was still moping about the loss of her ring. "I'll help you look again when I come back, Bonnie," Kelly offered. She hurriedly removed her makeup and jumped into her street clothes. Then she grabbed her coat and bag and made a dash for the door.

As Kelly approached the reception desk at her hotel, the desk clerk greeted her with a smile. "Did Mademoiselle have a good morning?"

"Yes, thank you." Kelly barely managed a smile in return, she felt so abandoned. Eric was nowhere in sight. "I, uh . . . wonder if you can tell me a little more about my friend. He didn't leave word where he was going, did he?"

The clerk looked at her sympathetically. "One minute, Mademoiselle," he said. Kelly saw him motion to the doorman. She prayed that the doorman had seen where Eric went. The two men conferred for a while, and then the desk clerk returned. Kelly tried to look as calm as possible, pretending she didn't really care that much.

"I have good news for you, Mademoiselle." The clerk smiled, giving her a tiny wink. "The doorman saw your friend go into Le Café de Milan. It is just down the street."

It took Kelly only a second to call out, *"Merci!"* before she was off. A few minutes later, she was walking into the restaurant. A slight snow had fallen that morning, making it very bright outside. The windows of the café were hung with heavy drapes, and it took Kelly's eyes a moment to adjust to the darkness. When she recovered her sight, she saw Eric immediately, sitting in a corner of the room near the kitchen. But he was sitting with . . . Nathalie!

"Kelly!" Eric jumped up when he saw her. "I thought you couldn't get away for lunch! What a surprise. But how did you know where to find us?"

"It wasn't too hard," Kelly replied coolly.

"Though I am surprised to see you here," she said, looking at Nathalie.

Nathalie laughed good-naturedly. "Really, Kelly, this is not one of those soap operas you Americans are forever watching. There is nothing sneaky going on here." She smiled at Eric. "Is there *chéri?*"

Eric gave Kelly a look she didn't understand as he explained, "Nathalie was nice enough to tell me you were working a little late and couldn't make it."

"I see," Kelly said slowly. "By the way, Nathalie, what were you doing in the lobby of the Hotel Gabriel at lunchtime, anyway?"

Nathalie jumped up, in a huff. "There happen to be a few other people staying at the Hotel Gabriel besides you. It wasn't built in your honor, you know."

"Like who?" Kelly said calmly.

"Like a very important film director, that is who!" Nathalie grabbed her coat. "I do not have to entertain small-town American boys for my amusement—even when *they* invite *me* to lunch!"

Kelly watched in amazement as Nathalie marched out of the restaurant, leaving Eric scowling at the closed door. The other patrons looked up from their meals. A flustered waiter picked up the napkin Nathalie had dropped in her hasty departure.

"Great—nice scene, Kelly," Eric said, shaking his head. "I hope you didn't ruin everything."

She sank into the chair Nathalie had just vacated. "Ruin what? Eric, please tell me the truth. Are you interested in Nathalie?"

For a moment, Eric just stared at Kelly.

"Don't look at me that way," she said, squirming.

Eric gaped at her. "Are you kidding? After the lunch I just had with Nathalie, you ask if I'm interested in her? Phew, now there's someone to feel sorry for."

"I don't get it—what are you talking about?"

Eric pulled a slim pad of paper from his jacket pocket. "Just a minute," he told her, scribbing hurriedly. When he had covered a page with notes, he looked up and put his pen aside. "There—I didn't want to forget any important parts."

Kelly was completely perplexed. "Eric, what's going on?"

Eric laughed lightly, taking Kelly's hands in his. "I guess you might be confused. You see, I was really intrigued by that story you told me, about Nathalie taking Bonnie's ring. I don't know, it just got to me—a beautiful girl, already a successful model and starting a new film career, and yet she steals another girl's engagement ring."

Kelly shook her head, mystified. "But what does that have to do . . ."

"Hold on." Eric took a sip of water. "You

forget—my uncle Didier is a journalist. I told him the story, and he gave me some advice. First of all, he said, never make accusations until you're certain of your facts."

"I agree with that . . ."

"Right. And second, don't scare off a source. Uncle Didier said the best way to get information out of someone is to befriend them. Show a genuine interest. You know, butter them up a little bit."

Slowly the light began to dawn. "You mean," Kelly said, "that you were trying to get Nathalie to trust you, so she'd open up to you?"

"You've got it. I don't think she'd actually admit she took the ring, but she told me enough about herself that I think I can make a pretty good guess." Eric laughed. "Maybe I've found a career for myself. This investigative journalism stuff is pretty interesting."

Kelly couldn't believe her ears. "Eric, you were a little *too* good. You nearly had me convinced that you liked Nathalie."

He was genuinely surprised. "But you know I . . ." Suddenly he squeezed her hand. "Hey, you know how I feel about you."

"Well, I thought I did." Kelly felt suddenly foolish. "But you said yourself, Nathalie is so pretty and all . . ."

"She's pretty, I guess, but I'd never be interested in someone like her. You didn't really think . . ." He chuckled. "I can't believe you were really worried that she could take your place."

"I wasn't really . . . but about . . . last night . . . at the hotel . . ." She faltered. "In the elevator . . . I'm sorry I was so rude."

"I thought you were a little cranky. But you get that way sometimes, especially when you've been working too hard."

Kelly stared at him helplessly, and Eric laughed out loud. "Come on, who could compete with you? I know you, Kelly, and you know me, better than anyone. And you still like me, too."

Kelly leaned her head on his shoulder, laughing with relief. "I did it again," she gasped. "I jumped to conclusions and made up my mind . . ."

"Before you knew the facts," Eric finished. "That's why you'd better leave the investigative reporting to me. Now let me tell you what I found out."

"Wait," Kelly said. "If you didn't go back to the nightclub last night, and you didn't arrange to meet Nathalie for lunch today, then how . . ."

"She told you," Eric said simply. "I bumped into her in the hotel lobby. You know, Kelly, she doesn't always lie. She may be a flirt and a real pain sometimes, but she isn't evil or anything. Sometimes, I think she even means well."

"I know," Kelly admitted. "She thought I was

being nice to her this morning, and she thanked me for it. But I just ignored her. I couldn't believe she was sincere."

"From what she told me, that's been the story of her life." Eric ordered Kelly an omelet, then gave her a quick rundown on everything Nathalie had told him. "First of all, she *was* in the hotel to meet a film director. She's desperate for another movie part. She's afraid she's a has-been at twenty. She brags about the movies she made, but even she admits they didn't amount to much."

"That's what I heard," Kelly agreed.

"Yeah, and this director guy stood her up; left town without even letting her know. She was in pretty bad shape with I bumped into her, and yet she made a big point of telling me you couldn't get away for lunch."

"Naturally. She wanted you to herself."

"Believe it or not, I think she likes you, Kelly. She told me so that I wouldn't think you'd stood me up. And I was the one who invited her out— that was the truth, too."

Kelly sank lower in her chair. "Now I feel awful," she exclaimed. "But you can't blame me. She *was* flirting with you last night. She would still try to steal you away from me, I know it."

"Maybe. But don't you feel sorry for her, anyway? I do."

Kelly ate a forkful of omelet. "Tell me more."

"She's really insecure. I guess she doesn't get

along with people, so she's very suspicious of them, especially other girls."

"I can see why," Kelly drawled.

"Anyway, get this—she told me that when she was a little girl, sometimes she took things, to get attention."

Kelly almost dropped her fork. "She said that?"

"And she might have said more, but unfortunately, that's when you came in."

"Barged in, you mean." Kelly eyed Eric thoughtfully. "You must have the magic touch. She sure told you a lot about herself."

"I asked a lot of questions. And I was interested, that's all."

"Okay," Kelly said, rolling her eyes and grinning. "I agree you're a genius. But what do we do now?"

Eric picked up his notebook. "I don't know. From what I told him even before I talked to her, Uncle Didier thought Nathalie might have some serious problems. You know, being insecure and competitive and all. She certainly could use more self-confidence. Anyway, he thinks we shouldn't get too involved, and that maybe she should talk to a professional counselor."

"How am I going to tell her that?" Kelly wondered. "I don't think Nathalie even knows she has a problem."

Eric shrugged. "I don't know, Kelly. But I

think Uncle Didier is right. We can't really do anything about it."

Kelly let out a big sigh. "But doing nothing won't help Bonnie. If it was me, and I had to tell my boyfriend I'd lost my engagement ring . . ."

Eric placed his hand over hers. "Somehow, I think your boyfriend might understand."

Kelly smiled. "Is that more flattery? Because seriously, Eric, I have to do something. I'm the only one who knows Nathalie may have the ring. I'm the only one who can help Bonnie. I've got to do something."

"Detective Eric advises you to be careful."

Kelly laughed. "You're turning into a real investigative reporter, aren't you?"

"Yes, and I was pretty good at it. Smooth, too. Nathalie never suspected a thing."

Kelly made a face. "Don't be so sure of yourself."

Eric raised his eyebrows. "I'll be glad when this whole thing is cleared up," he told her. "Then maybe I'll have you to myself again."

"That," Kelly said, "is the best idea I've heard all day."

Nine

Back at the studio, Patrick continued to shoot at a furious pace. He did his best to rev up everybody's energy using his usual method—yelling insults while they took their turns on the set. Lack of sleep and the day's events had taken their toll on everyone. Inge seemed to be in a kind of stupor. Bonnie spent the afternoon silently battling to keep back her tears. After one resentful look at Kelly, Nathalie remained quiet the rest of the day. Kelly was desperate for a plan, for some way to clear up the ring mystery and still have time for Eric. *Tomorrow is my last full day in Paris*, she realized. Tomorrow was New Year's Eve day, and at two o'clock on the following afternoon, New Year's Day, she would be flying home. Eric and his family would follow a few days later. *Tomorrow night will be the climax of my stay here in Paris!* It had to be absolutely perfect! She was going to have dinner with the Powerses as soon as the Bonjour assignment let out.

While Bonnie and Nathalie were on the set doing doubles, Kelly daydreamed about the dinner at the Des Barres apartment.

Eric's aunt Cecile loved candles, so she imagined the apartment filled with them: candles on the cherry mantle of the fireplace, candles on every table, ledge, and dresser in the house. Mrs. Powers and Cecile were going to make a huge turkey, with all the trimmings. And naturally there would be other courses: fish, paté, cheeses, salads, and desserts. They would probably eat until almost midnight. And then would come the magic moment when this year would turn into next year. The lights would dim and everyone would raise a glass and toast each other into the New Year. And then, the most wonderful moment of all: she and Eric would vow that this new year would be different than all the years before, because this year, they would really be a couple.

"What time is it?" Inge spoke for the first time that afternoon.

Kelly looked at the watch she had taken off and

put on the dressing-room counter. "It's close to six. I am *so* tired. I sure wish we could all go home!"

"Me, too." Inge turned to her in agreement. "But they have to get all the pictures done by this time tomorrow. That's when the booking ends."

"I know," Kelly said, toying with one of Tristan's makeup brushes. "But they sure loaded us with shots. I thought this was going to be a laid-back little Christmas booking."

Inge gave her a weak smile. "The Bonjour people are famous for being slave drivers. But still, I flew from Sweeden and you flew all the way from the United States to do this booking. And if we hadn't, there would've been a thousand other girls only too eager to take our places."

"And as soon as it's over, we'll probably forget all the bad parts, and only remember the good things."

Inge tried to smile. "Let's hope so," she finally said.

A minute later, Nathalie and Bonnie came back from their shoot. They began to remove their clothes and accessories; miniskirts, huge over-sized jackets, black-and-white patent-leather pumps, and horn-rimmed glasses.

They were barely dressed at all when Patrick burst into the room. "Everybody into the Marilyn Monroe dresses! Hurry up! We have several more shots before we break tonight!"

A unified groan went up among the girls. "Give us a break," Nathalie spoke up. "We have been working hard all day. We need a rest!"

The other girls murmured in agreement. Patrick looked from one to the other. "Ah—so my models feel overworked, eh? Maybe your agents should be aware of the problem!" With that, he stormed out of the dressing room.

"He's not going to call Simone, is he?" Kelly said worriedly. That was the last thing she needed.

Bonnie picked up a nail file. "He's being ridiculous! He's not going to call my agent in London over this."

Inge put in, "Mine's in London, too. But ridiculous or not, he might do it. Don't forget, he's as tired and as cranky as we are!"

"I guess you should know about that." Nathalie looked at her. Inge blushed red and looked away.

"Well, our agents wouldn't listen to a lot of rubbish from Patrick," Bonnie said. "They must know him pretty well, too." Kelly hoped Bonnie was right. One complaint from Simone and Meg might end her overseas bookings forever.

They got ready as quickly as possible, but not quickly enough for Patrick. He paced back and forth, fretting about the costumes, fretting about the makeup, fretting about the set. The models were all posed around an antique settee. Bonnie and Inge sprawled on the satin brocade sofa, while Kelly and Nathalie stood at either end, holding difficult poses and clasping giant feathers that had been dyed to match their dresses. In keeping with the Marilyn Monroe theme, they were all wearing identical blond wigs.

Secretly, Kelly thought the wigs looked ridiculous. Tristan had done his best to alter each girl's coloring, but only Inge and Bonnie, who were blonds, looked remotely natural in their wigs. Kelly and Nathalie, the darker two, looked totally artificial. Kelly doubted the Bonjour people would approve, but no one in the studio said a word. Everyone was afraid of Patrick's temper.

"No, no," Patrick screamed. "That is terrible! You all look like you are falling asleep."

"Maybe we are," Nathalie cracked, stifling a yawn.

"Stop that! Pay attention! Look alive!" He peered through the camera, but just as he clicked the shutter, Bonnie suddenly screamed.

"Ow—my foot," she yelled. "Oh, it's the most awful cramp!"

Patrick almost threw the camera at her, tripod and all. "Fine, now you have ruined the first good shot of the afternoon!"

"It wasn't her fault," Kelly said indignantly. "She has a cramp, for goodness' sake!"

"You are all against me," Patrick raved, running his hands through his hair, making himself look even more like a madman. Nathalie giggled, which only made Patrick angrier.

"But, *chéri*," Nathalie cajoled him, "you are not angry with little Nathalie."

"Be quiet," Patrick roared. "If I hear another word out of any of you, I will . . ." His face turned red as he sputtered vague threats.

The girls took their positions again, and Fabian finally had Patrick calmed down enough to take his place at the camera.

"That is better," Patrick said, trying to stay cool. "Fine, Bonnie, turn to your left some more . . . Good. Inge, darling, please, take the frown off your face."

Inge gave him a sick smile.

"That is terrible . . . I mean, that is fine, you look wonderful."

At last things seemed to be going well.

"Nathalie," Patrick continued, "put one hand on your hair, that's it. Now, tilt your head back . . . Dreamy expression, please . . . Fine, a little farther, farther . . ."

"*O, là là!*" Nathalie's blond wig fell onto the floor with a soft thud. There was a moment of total, complete silence—everyone tensed, waiting for an explosion from Patrick. And then, to Kelly's amazement, Nathalie sputtered and then burst out laughing. Kelly suddenly laughed, too, then Bonnie, and finally even Inge lost control. They all had the giggles. Overtired and tense, the silly scene got to everyone—everyone but

Patrick. The more helplessly they laughed, the angrier he became.

"Stop it! Stop," he screamed, more and more flustered. "All of you, listen to me. Pay attention!" He clapped his hands together like a dog trainer. "Listen to me!"

No one paid the least bit of attention.

Patrick picked up the phone. "I will call your agents," he threatened. "None of you will ever work again! I will say you are incompetent . . . unprofessional . . ."

Trying to stop laughing, Nathalie picked up the blond wig from the floor and dusted it off. "For goodness' sake, Patrick, it was an accident."

Patrick stared at her as if he'd never seen her before. "You—" he screamed, "you troublemaker! It is all your fault—everything is always your fault!"

Nathalie froze, then dropped the wig as if it were on fire. "If that is how you feel," she said, her voice as clipped and cold as Patrick's was wild and out of control, "you can finish this job without me. I have had enough of your insults."

With that, she stormed into the dressing room. Suddenly Inge was on her feet. "I've had enough, too," she declared. "I'm taking a break, and I'm not coming back until you apologize to all of us."

Kelly stared in amazement. She'd never expected to hear Inge take a stand about anything, least of all Patrick.

Patrick walked slowly over to the telephone, picked up the receiver, and dialed.

In the dressing room, the girls gathered around Inge. Clearly, she was as fed up with Patrick as any of them—*probably more so*, Kelly thought wryly. Bonnie was glad for the extra time in the dressing room. She got right onto her hands and knees, scouring every corner of the room one more time for the missing ring.

Kelly didn't mind the break, either. At this point, she didn't even care whether or not Simone believed Patrick's story. She'd had it.

"I'll just be glad when this whole thing is over," she complained, putting her feet up on the counter. Only Tristan seemed worried. He flitted from one girl to another, anxiously dabbing at their makeup with a tissue.

"This is the worst," he said anxiously. "This is a disaster! Nathalie, *chérie*, couldn't you have kept your mouth shut?"

"That is right, blame me." Nathalie pouted. "Everyone always blames me, no matter what I do."

The rest of the girls were silent. Kelly wondered if any of them felt sorry for Nathalie; she was beginning to feel more sympathetic toward the girl.

Simone was at the studio within twenty minutes of Patrick's call. She burst into the dressing room, her face red both from the late December cold and her anger.

"So?" she said hotly. "I hear you girls have decided to stage a strike. This is a fine thing for the reputation of FLASH!, Mademoiselles Kelly and Nathalie. Bonjour is one of our best clients!"

"Nobody's staging a strike, Simone," Kelly spoke up. "Patrick's exaggerating. It's just that we've been working so hard all day, and we're completely exhausted."

"Is that not peculiar." Simone raised an eyebrow. "Why is such a young, healthy girl so tired?"

Kelly looked defensive. "I'm just tired, that's all. We all are."

"But you especially," Simone said accusingly. "What time were you in bed last night?"

"I . . . uh . . . early. I can't remember exactly," Kelly stuttered. All eyes were on her.

Simone's mouth was set. "I happen to have a good friend who enjoys hearing rock music late at night, Kelly. And she said she saw a girl at La Boîte de Cave whose description matches yours." Kelly's face turned red.

Inge stepped up. "Who told you that?" the blond asked coolly.

"A friend," Simone retorted.

Both Inge and Bonnie turned to Nathalie—it was clear what they were thinking.

Nathalie looked hurt. "Do not look at me. I never said a word."

Simone caught on immediately. "So, Nathalie

—I guess that explains your own fatigue. You were out late also."

"Please, Simone." Nathalie pouted. "I am twenty years old. So I went out—it was just this once, and just for a little while. Do not be angry!"

Simone *was* angry, and she turned to Kelly, furious. "Then you *were* out late last night, young lady. You have a lot of explaining to do. But do not waste your breath with me. It is Meg Dorian who is going to get the real story."

Kelly's heart plunged. There was no way to get out of this one. Inge and Bonnie were lucky. Patrick didn't appear to have placed calls to London.

"Don't be so blind, Simone," Inge said, calm as ever. "Can't you see what's going on?"

"What do you mean?" Simone said.

"I mean, your friend obviously saw someone else, not Kelly. Nathalie just doesn't want to take all the blame. Actually, I was at the club, too. Kelly wasn't there. As she says, she was at her hotel, sound asleep."

"That's right," Bonnie said, leaping into the discussion. "I was there, too. We all were, every one of us—even Patrick."

Kelly's jaw dropped. What was going on? Bonnie was nowhere near that club last night!

"Patrick?" Simone screamed, outraged. "This is the last straw!" She rushed into the studio and confronted the photographer. Their voices could be heard above the loud rock music that someone had discreetly turned even louder. As the models listened, the heated debate got steadily more intense in volume and content.

Meanwhile, in the dressing room, Kelly was completely perplexed. "What are you all doing? Inge, why did you lie for me? You know I was at the club. And Bonnie, you weren't there at all! Why did you say you were?"

"Because we're all fed up, that's why!" Bonnie answered. "Everything's gone wrong on this shoot from the very beginning. I don't care if Simone gets mad—she isn't my agent. Anyway, I feel I owe you some help. You've tried to help me find my ring."

"Yes," Inge agreed. "You've been nice to all of us. You helped me get away with Patrick last night at the club, when I desperately needed to talk to him alone."

Nathalie scoffed. "Was he so eager for your company?"

Inge stepped close to Nathalie. "I'm tired of your snide little remarks, Miss Prima Donna. Why don't you come off your high horse?"

Nathalie was furious. "How dare you speak to me like that?"

"I've never met anyone like you," Inge declared. "Imagine inviting yourself along on a private date. You had no business being with

Patrick and me last night, Nathalie. Why are you always tagging along when you're not wanted?"

Nathalie turned her back on all of them, but Kelly could see her face in the mirror, and to her surprise, Nathalie's eyes were filled with tears. So Eric was right. She wasn't as tough as she pretended to be. She *did* care what others thought about her.

"No one is ever nice to me," Nathalie said coldly, not betraying her true feelings. "Why should I be nice to any of you?"

"You wouldn't know how," Bonnie declared. "Come on, Inge. I could use a nice cup of tea right now."

"I'm coming with you," Tristan said, following Bonnie through the curtains.

"Good idea," Inge said, listening to the sounds of Patrick and Simone's argument in the studio. "Only make mine coffee. Coming, Kelly?"

"No . . . you go ahead." Kelly pretended to search through her bag. In a moment, the dressing room was quiet. Nathalie still stood facing the mirror.

Nathalie's voice rang out, accusatory and angry. "Why do you not go with your friends? I do not want you here!"

"Maybe I want to be here."

"Why? You hate me, do you not? You all hate me." Nathalie's voice was cold.

"Nobody hates you, Nathalie," Kelly said

evenly. "If they're angry with you, it's because you treated them badly. Can't you see that?"

Nathalie made a scornful, disbelieving sound that almost ended Kelly's determination to be patient and sympathetic—like a good investigative reporter. She smiled to herself, thinking of Eric using that phrase.

"Do not laugh at me," Nathalie screamed, misinterpreting Kelly's grin. "I am sick and tired of people laughing at me behind my back!"

Kelly realized her mistake and quickly changed her expression. "Nobody's laughing at you, Nathalie. Why would they? They might envy you, but not laugh."

"Oh, sure," Nathalie snorted in disbelief.

"Well, it's true," Kelly insisted. "You have everything a girl could want. You're beautiful and you're very clever. You've already been in two films. Who knows where your career could take you?"

Nathalie quieted a bit. "Perhaps I am just touchy because I have more to lose than the other girls."

"Actually," Kelly said simply, "I never thought of it that way, but you know, you're right. You do have a lot to lose."

Nathalie's eyes narrowed suspiciously. "Why are you doing this? Why are you in here with me, anyway? You are worried about your boyfriend, are you not? You think I am going to take him away. Well, do not worry, I am not interested."

"It isn't that. Eric told me what happened, that he invited you to lunch. I'm not jealous of that."

"You are not?" Nathalie looked at her in surprise. "Well, then, you are very different from most girls."

"No, not really," Kelly said. "I just happen to know Eric very well, and I trust him completely."

"Naturally, you are a match made in heaven," Nathalie said cynically.

Kelly bit her lip. This was tougher than she'd imagined, and infinitely more trying. Nathalie was not easy to like. "Look, Nathalie, can we stop sniping at each other? It's . . . it's a real bore."

Nathalie seemed amused. Kelly felt a moment of despair—this wasn't getting her anywhere. There was so little time left to find out about Bonnie's ring. She tried a different approach.

"Nathalie, I just wanted to tell you . . . well, I think I understand how hard it must be for you sometimes. I know people do envy you, and probably act mean to you because of it. I guess that would make anyone a little, well, defensive—or make them act mean in return . . ."

"Do not feel sorry for me," Nathalie said sharply. "I do not need your pity. No one has to feel sorry for me."

"I don't feel sorry for you." Kelly almost gave up. But she couldn't tell Eric she'd gotten this far and then had blown the whole thing. She decided to give it one more try.

"Listen, Nathalie, I don't feel sorry for you. Why should I? The one I feel sorry for is Bonnie."

"Oh, Bonnie," Nathalie said in disgust.

"Yes, Bonnie." Kelly refused to back down. "I would hate to be in her place when she tells her fiancé her ring is gone."

"Then she should not have been so careless."

Kelly shrugged. "Maybe she wasn't careless."

"What do you mean?" Nathalie asked curtly. "Are you suggesting . . ."

"I'm not suggesting anything," Kelly said, keeping her voice as casual as she could. "Anything is possible. Who knows how it happened? Maybe someone did take it, I don't know. People take things for different reasons."

"What kind of reasons?" Nathalie said, as if she wasn't in the least bit interested.

"Well, I'm not sure, but I think sometimes people take things just to get attention, or to make themselves feel better. You know, like when you're little. Sometimes your friends get anything they ask for, but your parents are really strict and say you can't have the same things. It's not right to take things then, but it's human. Nobody's perfect."

"I do not think that is right at all," Nathalie said.

"Maybe not. But you hear all the time about

the things people do to get attention. For all I know, Bonnie never lost the ring. Maybe she just said so to get our attention."

"So we would all feel sorry for her," Nathalie added. "That would be stupid. I know I hate having people feel sorry for me."

"But that's the way you feel about someone who . . . does things to get attention." Kelly took a deep breath. Nathalie was beginning to open up, but one wrong word could ruin everything. "Maybe," Kelly said, as if they were playing a game, "maybe someone was mad at Bonnie. I mean, she was bragging about her ring and her fiancé an awful lot."

"She certainly was," Nathalie said calmly. "She was bragging about her wonderful love life, and . . . and at the same time, poor Inge had nothing but boyfriend troubles. Inge could have taken her ring out of anger or spite."

"You're right," Kelly said, although she felt nothing but confused. What if she was wrong, and *Inge* was the one who had taken Bonnie's ring?

"Sometimes," Nathalie continued, "things are not as they appear." She shrugged indifferently. "For instance, what if someone took the ring without meaning to."

"I don't understand," Kelly said.

"What if someone just wanted to take a closer look at it, because Bonnie had left it carelessly lying around. What if they even meant to put it in a safe place, but before they could, someone barged in on them and put them in a very embarrassing position?"

Kelly remembered every detail of the moment when she'd walked into the dressing room and found Nathalie going through the bags. With a shock, she realized it might have happened exactly the way Nathalie just said. Suppose Nathalie had meant only to admire the ring, and then to put it in a safe place for Bonnie, but instead, Kelly walked in and caught her.

"If that happened," Kelly said slowly, "why wouldn't the person simply explain that they'd meant no harm?"

"Perhaps no one would have believed that person," Nathalie answered. "Perhaps no one ever believes that person. Everyone is not forgiving and understanding. Some people are very nasty, and very jealous."

Kelly was silent. Everything Nathalie had said sounded so logical. If only she knew for sure. At this point, she was beginning to doubt her own instincts.

She gave Nathalie a look of grudging admiration. The girl certainly wasn't stupid. In fact, she wished Nathalie were less complex.

Quietly, she said, "Whatever happened, it's been terrible for Bonnie, and I think that

. . . well, that no matter who took the ring, maybe they need professional help."

Nathalie's face burned red and a look of disgust spread across her face. Instantly, Kelly regretted her words.

"You are so superior, are you not?" Nathalie cried. "You think you know it all." She thrust her face close to Kelly's. "If you ask me, you are the one who needs help."

At that moment, the dressing-room curtains were thrown aside and Inge, Bonnie, and Tristan hurried in.

"I can't believe they're still talking out there," Bonnie said. "They barely noticed that we left and came back!" She looked from Kelly to Nathalie. "What did we miss?"

Luckily, Kelly didn't have to answer. Patrick and Simone chose that moment to enter the dressing room.

"You are all dismissed," Patrick yelled, his face flushed with anger. "Go home to your beds and get your precious beauty rest. Beat it!"

Kelly felt a ray of hope. "Are we coming back tomorrow?"

"Yes, you are," Simone said coldly. "Thank you, Patrick."

Everyone scrambled around packing their bags, throwing on coats.

Inge hurried over to Simone. "Thank you," she said. "I'm so glad to go home."

"Yes, me, too," Bonnie added happily. "I've had it. Cheerio!"

Simone turned to Kelly and Nathalie and glowered at them. Bonnie and Inge paused at the door. "Calling a strike is not exactly good for the agency's reputation," she said. "Nathalie, how could you pull a stunt like this? I will deal with you later. And both of you are on strict curfew tonight. That means you, too, Kelly. No night-clubs, is that clear?"

Kelly felt terrible. "Wait," she said, so loudly everyone was startled. "I have a confession to make." She swallowed hard. "About last night . . . well, I was there. I was at that club. I'm as guilty as Nathalie for what happened today."

Simone exploded in rage once again. "Then you all lied to me! Kelly Blake, you are not to leave that hotel room for anything. I will call every hour on the hour, I will come to check the room myself. And do not think I am kidding!"

"I don't," Kelly said with a weary smile. "I believe you."

Simone, still sputtering with rage, stormed out of the studio, slamming the door behind her.

"That was really dumb," Nathalie told her, shaking her head. "You have so little time left in Paris, and now you cannot see your boyfriend at all tonight."

"I know," Kelly said with a sigh. "But it wasn't fair to you for me not to be punished. It was a lie."

"Your noble sacrifice does not impress anyone," Nathalie said.

Inge laid a hand on Kelly's arm in sympathy. "I understand why you did it," she said.

Bonnie clucked her tongue. "Too bad," she said, "now you can't see Eric, and it's your own fault."

It was her own fault, Kelly knew that. And the haughty look in Nathalie's eyes as they all parted for the night made her wonder if she'd just made one of the most useless gestures of her life.

Ten

When Kelly got back to her hotel, it was only eight o'clock. If she'd felt tired at the shoot, she felt half dead as she entered the elevators. Once in her room, she lifted the phone and dialed Eric's number. His aunt answered.

"Hi, Madame des Barres, it's Kelly. Kelly Blake."

"Ah. *Bonsoir*, Kelly. How are you?"

"Fine. And you?" Kelly was in no rush to speak to Eric and tell him the bad news about their evening.

"Fine, thank you. I'll get Eric," Cecile said.

The few seconds that passed seemed like hours to Kelly.

"Hello? Kelly?" Eric said.

"Eric? I have terrible news. I don't have the evening off."

"Oh, no! What happened?"

"I'm—I'm being punished."

"Punished? You mean, like, sent to your room?"

"I know, I know, it sounds ridiculous, but there was a huge fight at the studio today." She filled Eric in on everything that had happened. "I really made a mess of it, didn't I?"

"What were you trying to do, anyway?"

"I don't know. I guess I had this idea that if I made Nathalie feel that I trusted her, she might tell me what happened."

"In one conversation? You thought she'd be your best friend and admit she stole the ring?"

Kelly fiddled with the phone cord. "I guess that was pretty stupid of me."

"No, not stupid," Eric said hastily. "You meant well. But I hope you didn't scare her off."

"I purposely kept things very vague, as if I were talking about someone else. In fact, at one point, she had me convinced Inge took the ring, or even Bonnie herself, just to get attention."

When she explained more fully, Eric whistled softly. "Wow, Nathalie's pretty sharp. Now I'm not sure, either, if she took the ring."

"I know," Kelly moaned. "Not only am I a

failure as a detective, but I couldn't help Bonnie. And worst of all, I ruined our night together. What a mess."

"Don't feel too bad. I think you were on the right track."

"Yeah, but I stuck my nose into other people's business, and I only ended up hurting myself. When am I ever going to learn?"

"Hey, don't be too hard on yourself," Eric said softly. "Some people still think you're pretty special."

"Oh, yeah?" Kelly kept her tone light. "Who?"

"Guess."

"Well, maybe I have a pretty good idea who you mean," she teased.

"Why don't you think about it overnight. Tomorrow, I'll let you know for sure who it is."

"Okay. But what do I get if I guess right?"

"Wait and see," Eric chuckled.

Kelly wished she could stay on the phone with Eric forever, but she was afraid Simone might try to call, and she knew the agent would be furious if Kelly's line was busy all night.

"It's a deal," she told Eric softly. "See you tomorrow."

It was business as usual at the studio the next morning, even though it was New Year's Eve.

"Bonjour!" Patrick greeted Kelly as she rushed through the door.

"Bonjour," she replied, staring at his cheerful face in amazement.

"What's with Patrick?" she asked Bonnie in the dressing room. "He's so cheerful this morning."

Bonnie hardly bothered to look up. "That's Patrick. When he's good, he's good. But when he's bad, he's rotten."

Kelly smiled. "Any sign of your ring, Bonnie?"

"Don't even mention it," Bonnie said gloomily. "Looks like I'm going to have to go back to England without it. I don't know how I'm going to explain it to Derek."

"There's still time," Kelly offered. "I have a strong feeling it's going to turn up."

"Do you?" Bonnie brightened at this. "You know, losing that ring is the worst thing that ever happened to me."

"Bonjour." Nathalie breezed into the room, pulled off her scarf and flung it onto an empty chair. "Everybody got a good night's sleep last night, I hope?"

"Yes, I guess we all had to," Inge cracked, and Bonnie and Kelly laughed. For an instant, Nathalie tensed, but when she realized no one was laughing at her, she joined right in.

"Actually, I didn't," Bonnie replied. "I was too worried. I wish I felt rested. At least Patrick seems to be in a pretty good mood."

"Well, that's good," Nathalie commented. "Because we have to make up for all the shots we did not get to last night. It is going to be some day."

"In that case, I'm going to get a cup of tea now," Bonnie announced. "Tristan isn't here yet, and I probably won't get a chance later." She left the room.

"It's really a shame about Bonnie's ring, isn't it?" Inge commented. Nathalie was rummaging through her bag, putting her makeup brushes that she wanted Tristan to use onto the counter.

"Of course." Nathalie glanced at Kelly briefly. "Bonnie has probably been careless with it, but I expect it will turn up today."

Inge said, "Don't you know what Bonnie must be going through? Don't you ever care about anybody besides yourself?"

Nathalie put her bag down and stared at Inge. "Of course I care. But what do you expect me to do? Find the ring for her?"

Kelly saw her chance and quickly grabbed it. "We could all try," she said quickly.

"Yes, I suppose I could help look for it as well," Inge admitted. "Sorry, Nathalie."

Nathalie stared at her dumbly. "That is okay."

Bonnie came back with her tea. "Here, duckies," she announced cheerfully. "I got some for both of you, too. And a coffee for Inge."

"Thanks." Kelly took a cup from the makeshift

tray Bonnie held out to her. Nathalie took her tea, too, but she didn't even look at it.

"I'm so late!" Tristan flew into the dressing room. He threw his bag down and took out brushes and bottles, laying them in neat rows on the counter. "I hope Monsieur Patrick is in a good mood today. You all seem to be happy."

"He is." Bonnie sipped her tea. "Do you mind if I go first today?"

Inge nodded knowingly. "I guess you can't wait to leave here."

Bonnie made a face. "Yes, but I'm dreading going home. Unless I find that ring!"

"Hey!" Tristan called out. "Speaking of lost things, I'm missing my big powder brushes. Did anyone stick them in her bag by accident?" He looked over at the things Nathalie had spread out before the mirror. "*Chérie, chérie*—there you go again. You're always picking up my things by mistake. I'm going to have to label everything from now on!"

Nathalie colored, conscious of the other girls watching. "Tristan, it was an accident. You know that!" Nathalie gave the makeup man a kiss on the cheek, but Inge glanced up and caught Kelly's eye.

"Oh, uh, I used one of your brushes, too," Kelly said, holding up a brush. Nathalie turned and stared at her with dark, cold eyes.

* * *

Bonnie and Inge were made up first. They dressed and walked to the set, pulling at zippers and buttons.

Tristan· walked behind them, still teasing the back of Inge's hair. Kelly was left alone in the dressing room with Nathalie. The French girl lit a cigarette, though Kelly had never seen her smoke before. She guessed it was part of Nathalie's dramatic touch.

Nathalie looked at Kelly between puffs of smoke. "I know what you are thinking. You think I took Tristan's brushes on purpose."

Kelly shook her head. "I never said that."

"What happened just now with Tristan's brushes was an accident," Nathalie insisted. "If I had really stolen those brushes, do you think I would display them on the counter?"

Kelly just shrugged helplessly. Nathalie gave a deep sigh and changed the subject. "Patrick is so much better today. Perhaps he and Inge have made up."

"I guess," Kelly said. "It's hard to tell what's going on with those two."

Tristan came back into the dressing room. "Okay, Nathalie, you're next."

Nathalie stubbed out her cigarette and sat down at the counter. A few minutes later, Bonnie and Inge burst into the dressing room.

"Break time," Bonnie said gaily. "Patrick's readjusting the lighting."

"I can't believe his change of mood," Inge said.

"But, Inge," Nathalie blurted, "are you not dating him?"

Inge's mouth dropped open and a red flush crept up her neck. "I am not," she responded hotly. "Why does everybody think that? Just because I went with him once to that club? People see you with someone for one second, and then the rumors start. You know, things aren't always as they seem!"

"They certainly are not!" Nathalie said dryly. "I'm sorry, Inge." Kelly didn't miss the look Nathalie cast in her direction.

Kelly wavered. How did everything get so complex? She, too, had believed that Inge and Patrick were dating each other. And she had based that belief on the single fact that she had seen the two of them together in the club. But now it seemed she'd been wrong. Could she be wrong about Nathalie, too?

"There." Inge thrust a photograph under Nathalie's nose. "*This* is my boyfriend, if you want to know. His name is Lars." Kelly caught a glimpse of a boy as young and blond as Inge herself. Just as she'd pictured Inge's boyfriend before she became caught up in the intrigues at the shoot!

Nathalie studied the picture. "Ah, so I have been proven wrong. I could not imagine what you saw in Patrick, anyway. Lars looks like a nice guy."

"Girls, girls, girls!" Patrick burst into the room. "Break is over. Nathalie, please get dressed. Kelly, you are next for makeup."

The time flew by. There were triples, with three girls all together in one shot, and doubles, and more singles. Before Kelly knew it, it was six o'clock and the Bonjour job was finished. Tonight she would celebrate a happy New Year's Eve with Eric's family.

The girls began to pack their bags and get into their own clothes, chattering about their evening plans. Suddenly there was a startled yell.

"My ring—I've found my ring!" Bonnie held it up to the light.

"Where was it?" Inge wanted to know.

"Why—right here in the zipper compartment of my bag." Bonnie looked around, puzzled. "I'm sure I've been through the entire bag a million times."

"You never know," Inge commented. "Sometimes things can get caught in the seam. But I'm glad you found it, Bonnie."

"Me, too!" Bonnie breathed a sigh of relief. "When Derek picks me up at the airport tonight, I won't have to hide anything from him. What a way to start out the New Year!"

"I wish I could get a flight to Sweden tonight!" Inge sighed. "But I have to wait until tomorrow. Lars was so disappointed about my not being home for New Year's Eve!"

"Well, do not let it be a total loss," Nathalie offered. "Come spend New Year's Eve at my house, Inge. My family will be there too. I—I would like for you to meet them."

Inge looked startled. "I'd like that, Nathalie," she said quietly.

"So what are you going to do?" Nathalie turned to Kelly.

"I'm spending the evening with my boyfriend's family," she said, trying to keep her voice calm. "It'll be quiet, but fun, I think."

"Well, I hope it's a wonderful night," Bonnie said, throwing her arms around Kelly's shoulders and giving her a big squeeze. "You deserve it. Hey, maybe we'll work together again some-time—maybe you'll come to London, or I'll get a job in New York!"

"That would be great!" Kelly agreed. "And, Bonnie, good luck with Derek!"

Bonnie held the engagement ring up for every-one to see. The diamonds glinted and sparkled. "Thanks—but somehow I have a feeling I won't be so unlucky from now on! Cheerio!"

Everyone called good-bye to Bonnie as she rushed out of the studio. Now that the job was over and the pressure was off, everyone acted like the best of friends. It was just as Kelly had predicted; the bad times were already fading from memory. Kelly looked around at Patrick and Tristan, at Inge and Nathalie, and felt a rush of affection for all of them.

"In the spirit of the holiday," Patrick cried, "I wish you all the very best. You are wonderful models, though," he added, "perhaps a bit temperamental. No one could have done a better job."

Kelly and Inge and Nathalie exchanged amused looks. Then they all began to gather their belongings together. Kelly said her good-byes to the other girls with hugs and kisses.

As she headed for the studio door, Kelly heard Nathalie call her name.

"Kelly, wait," She rushed to Kelly, her eyes downcast. "I just wanted to say . . ." She rubbed a hand over her hair nervously. "Well, I just wanted to say that sometimes, you meet a friend in the strangest places."

"Good luck, Nathalie—with everything. I know you'll be a success!" Kelly said.

Nathalie shrugged. "We shall see," she said matter-of-factly. "I know I have the talent."

Kelly couldn't help smiling. No matter what happened, nothing could crimp Nathalie's brash style.

As her taxi sped toward her hotel, Kelly thought about Nathalie. She'd never know for sure if the French girl had taken Bonnie's ring; if she'd intended to steal it or had just been caught in an awkward situation; if Kelly's talk with her had played any part in the reappearance of the ring. *Nothing was easy about this trip!* she thought. *Even Eric was different from the way he is at home. But I'm glad he was.*

Now that the strain of the job was over, she had mingled feelings of relief and regret. She was eager to get back home to friends and family, but most of all, she was looking forward to New Year's Eve with Eric. In her hotel room was a brand-new, strapless, knee-length black velvet dress that she'd bought a few weeks before for the Christmas holidays. She could hardly wait for Eric to see her in it.

Madame des Barres had prepared an elaborate—and delicious—five-course meal. They were barely finished with dessert when the clock struck midnight.

Didier des Barres raised his glass. "Let us make a toast!" he announced. "To our families, both in America and in France!" Everyone cheered, and there were kisses all around. Eric stood up and took Kelly aside.

"I can do better than that. Let's start this year off right, Kelly." He smiled at her and took both her hands in his. "To us."

"I'll drink to that."

"No, not drink. Kiss," Eric corrected her. And then they were in each other's arms, kissing the New Year in. Kelly could only hope that every single moment of the year would be as wonderful as this.

ABOUT THE AUTHOR

YVONNE GREENE was born in the Netherlands and emigrated to the United States as a young girl. At seventeen, she began a successful international modeling career, which she still pursues today. She has been featured on the pages of all the major American and European fashion magazines. Ms. Greene is also the author of two best-selling Sweet Dreams novels, *Little Sister* and *Cover Girl*, and *The Sweet Dreams Model's Handbook*.

STARFIRE

Out of the Romantic Past Comes

THE
TEXAS
TRILOGY

Set against the wild backdrop of Texas in the 1860s, here
are three books, full of excitement and romance, about
three beautiful young women dealing with the harsh realities
of frontier life and reveling in the promise of love.

Strongwilled Maggie McNeill is determined to make a success of
the family ranch and win the heart of adventurous Buck Crawford.
A danger-filled 700-mile cattle drive becomes the scene of Maggie's
dramatic efforts.

DREAMS AT DAWN: THE TEXAS TRILOGY: BOOK I

Restless, impulsive Tayah, half-Apache, half-white, strikes out on
her own searching desperately for a place where she can belong.
Cleve Harmon knows Tayah's place is in his heart, but it's going to
take a lot to convince Tayah of that.

APACHE FIRE: THE TEXAS TRILOGY: BOOK II

Headstrong Charlotte Harmon, pampered and elegant, has to
work hard for the first time in her life when disaster strikes the
Harmon stables. And making an impression on the elusive Juan
Ortiz isn't easy either. But Charlotte is used to winning—nothing
is going to stand in her way.

HIDDEN LONGINGS: THE TEXAS TRILOGY: BOOK III

THE TEXAS TRILOGY
DREAMS AT DAWN: BOOK I APACHE FIRE: BOOK II HIDDEN LONGINGS: BOOK III

Coming soon wherever paperback books are sold.

It's the New Hit Series from Bantam Books that takes you behind the scenes of a T.V. Soap Opera.

Share the highs and lows, the hits and flops, the glamour and hard work, the glory and heartache of life on the **Soap Set with:**

| KATIE NOLAN | SHANA BRADBURY | MITCH CALLAHAN |

Each a star in their own right, each a seasoned professional aiming for the top, each a teenager dealing with the ups and downs, the crazy ins and outs of teenage life—all in the glaring light of the camera's all-seeing eye!

ALL THAT GLITTERS
It's Golden!

Look For:

MAGIC TIME: ALL THAT GLITTERS #1 (Coming in February 1987)

TAKE TWO: ALL THAT GLITTERS #2 (Coming in March 1987)

FLASHBACK: ALL THAT GLITTERS #3 (Coming in April 1987)

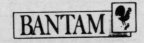

A LOVE TRILOGY
First there is <u>LOVING</u>.

Meet Caitlin, gorgeous, rich charming and wild. And anything Caitlin wants she's used to getting. So when she decides that she wants handsome Jed Michaels, there's bound to be some trouble. ☐ 24716/$2.95

Then there is <u>LOVE LOST</u>.

The end of term has arrived and it looks like the summer will be a paradise. But tragedy strikes and Caitlin's world turns upside down. Will Caitlin speak up and risk sacrificing the most important thing in her life?
☐ 25130/$2.95

And at last, <u>TRUE LOVE</u>.

Things are just not going the way Caitlin had planned, and she can't seem to change them! Will it take a disaster and a near-fatality for people to see the light?
☐ 25295/$2.95

Prices and availability subject to change without notice.

Buy them at your local bookstore or use this handy coupon for ordering:

Bantam Books presents a Super

Sweet Dreams

Surprise

Two Great Sweet Dreams Special Editions

Get to know characters who are just like you and your friends . . . share the fun and excitement, the heartache and love that make their lives special.

☐ 25884-2 MY SECRET LOVE: Special Edition #1 by Janet Quin-Harkin. Laura Mitchell's mother has big plans for her future as a belle of Texas high society. But Laura's interests lie elsewhere, especially when she falls in love with Billy-Joe, a poor boy. So far she's managed to keep their love a secret, but when he's falsely accused of a crime, only Laura can clear his name. $2.95

☐ 26168-1 A CHANGE OF HEART Special Edition #2 by Susan Blake. Shy, pretty Hilary Malone has always lived in the shadow of her older sister Amy. Concentrating on her painting leads Hilary into a special friendship with Jason Wolf. But even Jason's love may not be enough to relieve Hilary's conscience when Amy is injured in a tragic accident. $2.95
